Framework of the Human Body
Edited by Catherine Mwitta

framework of the human body

an anthology of writing about the human body and what it carries

edited by Catherine Mwitta

ISBN 978-1-7387167-1-5 (print) | ISBN 978-1-7387167-2-2 (ebook)

Edited by Catherine Mwitta
Cover art by Catherine Mwitta
Copyediting by Devon Field
Text design by Angela Caravan

LIBRARY AND ARCHIVES CANADA CATALOGUING IN PUBLICATION
Title: Framework of the human body : an anthology of writing about the human body and what it
   carries / edited by Catherine Mwitta.
Names: Mwitta, Catherine, editor.
Identifiers: Canadiana (print) 2022047625X | Canadiana (ebook) 20220476373 | ISBN 9781738716715
   (softcover) | ISBN 9781738716722 (EPUB) | ISBN 9781738716739 (Kindle)
Subjects: LCSH: Canadian literature—21st century. | LCSH: Human body—Literary collections. | CSH:
   Canadian literature (English)—21st century
Classification: LCC PS8237.H86 F73 2022 | DDC C810.8/03561—dc23

Bell Press publishes and operates on the unceded Coast Salish Territories of the Musqueam, Tsleil Waututh, and Squamish peoples.

Thank you to everyone who supported our Kickstarter to bring this book to life!

Extra special thanks to:

Linda & Mark Pickering
Tobias Toleman
Cathy Caravan

Trigger warning: this book engages with various perceptions, ideas, and biases about the human body. Some works discuss, engage with, or contain reference to fatphobia, eating disorders, body dysmorphia, sexual assault, physical violence, and suicide.

bellpressbooks.com
Twitter: @bellpressbooks
Instagram: @bellpressbooks

Contents

Introduction

I've been enamoured with the art of body modification since I was a child. The sting of a needle tattooing my skin or filling my lips with Juvéderm feels almost ritualistic. The cutting, bleaching and dyeing of my hair every three months also feels ceremonial. Monthly, I pull strips of wax paper off my legs. The result is a pair of smooth legs and a euphoric throbbing. Every day, I take eight supplements, one antibiotic and one antidepressant. My body is a temple or more like "a rotted peach," as Perfume Genius sings in "My Body." Sadly, the results of preening are purely aesthetic. I still hate my body.

How can we discover the meaning of life without first feeling it? In *Under the Skin* (2013), Scarlett Johansson is an extraterrestrial on earth who learns about the meaning of humanity. In the film's last scene, her human cover comes off and under it is the extraterrestrial's actual appearance. She's embraced her identity as a human. So, when the suit disappears, the extraterrestrial is devastated. She is vulnerable and bare. She can no longer hide her true self behind outfits, makeup and a coy smile. To survive in this world, we must constantly hide (protect) our true selves. But sometimes, hiding who we truly are does more damage than good. After all, *The Body Keeps the Score.*

Yet, this is a minor inconvenience considering I'm able-bodied. Last summer, I visited Vancouver city hall to write an article about a developer's rezoning application for 800-876 Granville Street. The first item on the agenda was Vancouver

City's Phase I Accessibility Strategy. City hall did not meet its year-end goal regarding the Phase I Accessibility Strategy. For over two hours, disabled citizens of Vancouver took the stand to tell their testimony about the lack of accessibility in the city. Disabled people are constantly undermined and overlooked, not only by the government but by their peers too. And when marginalized people choose not to be confined within oppressive societal expectations, they are vilified.

Nicole Byer, Aaron Rose Philip and Nyma Tang are some public figures that inspire me. When I was a teen, I cultivated my persona after women like Beyonce and Rihanna. However, I soon discovered that it was impossible to fake confidence until it covered my body like a steel casing. Even as my self-love grew, criticism about how I looked from family and friends still affected me. I realized that being confident wasn't a permanent state of being: self-love, self-confidence and self-esteem ebbs and flows. I will not say that confidence is ephemeral, but that I am merely human. Therefore, when a man tells me I'm too dark for them to love, or when my peers compare my afro to a clown wig it's natural for my ego to be hurt. What matters is my resiliency. My ability to rebuild myself back up each time I'm overlooked and underappreciated.

Take away the makeup and the clothes; underneath, I have a green mark on my butt, a scar on the bridge of my nose from a gardening accident and a mole on my cheek. In *No Longer Human* by Osamu Dazai, a young Japanese man, Oba Yozo, battles with whether to live a life following the traditions of his northern aristocratic Japanese family or the mainstream ideals of the western world. As he ruminates about his future, he states "now I have neither happiness nor unhappiness. Everything passes. That is the one and only thing that I have thought resembled a truth in the society of human beings where I have dwelled up to now as in a burning hell. Everything passes." This body shall, too, pass away one day. Our bodies will decompose, but what people will remember is the integrity of our character. I hope this anthology inspires you to reassess how you view your body and discover the unimaginable power it holds.

Sincerely,
Catherine Mwitta

Metamorphosis

by Teika Marija Smits

Author note:
This poem, about a tragic event in my life, required me to ven-
ture into my inner landscape to awaken dormant memories and
sleeping grief so that I could once again experience a particular
set of distressing and disorientating feelings. Allowing the discom-
forting emotions to rush through me, I did my best to grasp them
and contain their essence in words. An uncomfortable experience,
of course, but one which crystallised an event that, in essence,
changed me profoundly. I hope it speaks to those who have been in
a similar situation.

Foolishly, I'd wanted something exciting to happen,
for my adulthood to come sooner
rather than later.
{BREATHE IN}
But
when
my
father's death
triggered my
metamorphosis and I
found myself hauled up
by my feet, hanging upside down,
forever tethered to this moment
and cocooned in shock—
limbs, mouth, eyes, nose bound
in a glue of silk—the air squeezed
out of my teenage lungs,
powerless, mute,
digestive enzymes dissolving
my flesh as each bone snapped
and splintered, the pain
so exquisite, so intense…
{BREATHE IN} {BREATHE OUT}
…I realized how naive
I'd been, and I longed
for an end to it all. For
some unseen hand
to find me as
this chrysalis;
to crush
me to
death.

Teika Marija Smits is a UK-based writer and freelance editor whose poetry has appeared in a number of anthologies and magazines. Her debut poetry pamphlet, *Russian Doll*, was published by Indigo Dreams Publishing in March 2021. A fan of all things fae, she is delighted by the fact that Teika means fairy tale in Latvian.

teikamarijasmits.com @MarijaSmits

out of body

by Dawn Macdonald

oh I used to have
        a perfect body,
piscine-jointed, bones so
fine you'd choke. I wore
my shoulders like a cloak,
tossing one back, then
the pair, making
a line of my lats, standing
so my shadow would fly.

oh the body was perfect. my
dirt was musk, my calluses
were faerie-slippers, fitted
to the ball, and my scars were slim
ladies, presentable.
each had a little story
to introduce her. a prologue
to a kiss. each scar was a stanza
in a well-form'd sonnet hushed
between lovers' lips. a punch line
to an inside joke.

[m   o   n   t   a   g   e:

  d   e   c   a   d   e]

it isn't that I've got more scars,
nor that I'm older, true but not
the point. my body's stepped

                    aside

I'm not

following.

the falling out

by Dawn Macdonald

all my teeth have fallen out. my feet
have fallen out. I've floated
                              over power lines
unable to control my altitude,
which is a reason to keep
feet fastened.
                all my hair has fallen
out, and my hands, when I could not
operate a telephone.
                      the words we spoke
to each other then were worth remembering

most likely

Dawn Macdonald lives in Whitehorse, Yukon, where she was raised off the grid. She holds a degree in applied mathematics and used to know a lot about infinite series. Her poetry has appeared in over two-dozen journals and anthologies, and has been nominated for a Pushcart Prize.

Pluripotent

by J. W. Wood

for Cyrille

Claire's eyelids fluttered. Her fingers twitched, then she fell asleep.

Claire dreamed about Dave when he was young: that long black hair. Sonic Youth records and hand-rolled cigarettes. Turning up at anti-poverty marches promising to devote his medical skills to victims in war zones. And then what?

Claire opened her eyes. She thought she was still sleeping. Tiny figures danced on the blankets, aquamarine and shimmering. She rubbed her eyes and sat up. The little shapes played on the grey hospital blanket in front of her. A man and a woman, acting out a drama. She recognized them from somewhere.

"Do you remember when that was on TV?"

A voice by her bed. Claire leaned forward, seeking its source.

"Relax," the voice said. "You're still post-operative. We thought we'd show you a hologram of something popular from your day—a TV show."

"Oh," said Claire, her voice hoarse. She needed water. She found a half-full carafe on her bedside table, poured a glass and then drank it. She felt dizzy. She looked toward the voice. "So where am I, and what the hell's going on?"

"You will recall—or maybe not—signing a permission form when you were an undergraduate?"

She turned to her left. The voice belonged to a tall, slim man with greying hair. He wore an open-necked blue shirt and dark trousers. He sat at the foot of her bed, light from the bedside lamp glinting off a gold watch on his wrist.

"I did?"

The man nodded and smiled.

"You did, you and six classmates from undergrad biochemistry. The idea was to take a chemical snapshot of your synaptic activity, then reintroduce that to your brain twenty-five years later. It was a scientific experiment."

"You mean you've made me young again."

"Well, that's the idea. How do you feel, Dr. Hetman?"

"Dr. Hetman," Claire repeated.

"Right," he said. "Professor Hetman, in fact. You teach in this hospital. You're a clinical neuro-psychologist. You wanted this."

Claire let her head rest back on the pillow. She just wanted to sleep. And she preferred dreaming to the realization that reality wasn't what it used to be.

"Professor Hetman? Are you there?" the man asked, his face wrinkling in concern.

Claire wasn't sure if she knew where "there" was: she'd gone to sleep one night and awoke to find some middle-aged dweeb telling her she'd had her mind rinsed. She snickered. Middle-aged dweeb. A term straight from the '90s.

She looked down at her hands, their roadmap of veins, the carefully-tended nails and thick platinum wedding band studded with diamonds. The hands of a middle-aged woman.

"I'm married?" she asked with faint surprise.

The man sat on her bed and nodded, his eyes smiling. "Yes,

you are. Claire, it's me. Dave. Your husband. Has your memory completely gone?"

"Dave," she repeated, adding quickly: "Darling. Get me a mirror, could you?"

Dave reached for a mirror encased in white plastic on the bedside table. Claire felt fresh dizziness hit as she propped herself up on the pillows. Dave handed her the mirror.

"I thought this might be the first thing you'd ask for."

Claire looked in the mirror. Her hair was expensively cut and dyed, with the slightest hint of grey at the roots. Her face had aged most: eyes circled with stains of fatigue, cheeks drawn, skin sagging a little under her jaw.

"Do we have children?"

Dave made a pained expression.

"You don't remember anything, do you?"

Claire searched her memory. Nothing.

"What did I do? Where did the years go?"

Dave raised his eyebrows. "We both graduated pre-med and went to medical school. We deferred working for Médecins Sans Frontières until we'd paid off our loans. So we went into hospital work, and the shifts nearly killed us. After three years, we switched to family practice. Paying off our loans took longer than expected, even though we saved over half of every paycheck."

"Then what?"

Claire put the mirror down and looked at Dave, seeing the lines etched deep in his forehead for the first time. She saw the man she'd known long ago: older, yes, but grown. For good or bad, she couldn't tell. She tried to ignore the mild pain in her head and focus on what her newly-discovered husband was saying:

"We hit thirty and wanted children. So we had Jane and Mike. They're at school right now, but they'll come by later."

"And my Dad? Mum?"

"Claire—I …"

"Tell me."

Dave looked away, lamplight cutting into his worn features. Claire tried to focus. She remembered smoking weed and listening to Nirvana with Dave while he cursed George H. Bush. She remembered anti-apartheid marches, making love in a bedroom at some frat party. But her Dave had been lithe, tanned—not a wrinkled middle-aged man. Dave used to walk the three miles between their undergraduate dorms just to see if she was there. He would leave scribbled notes on the door, and her heart would soar when she saw them.

That was then. Right now, Claire had to decide what she would say next. See if she could make any connection, feel something out from the past—or did she mean the future? What if it had stayed in 1997 forever in her head?

"You know what, Dave? You still look hot," Claire smiled, reaching for his hand.

Dave's look was blank, passionless—above all, tired. The same ringlets of fatigue as her, a few more crow's feet.

"Claire. About your parents. Your father died ten years ago. Lymphoma. You were never the same after his death. You used to burst out crying every time you saw your uncle. Your mother lives with us: she forgets to flush the toilet sometimes. Calls me by your dad's name."

"And what about practising medicine in war zones?"

"Never happened after the kids came along."

"Do you still go on demos and stuff?"

"Get real. I'm a family doctor in a small town. Do you think I'd have any patients if I wore my politics on my sleeve?" Dave's face had darkness written in its lines. "I carried on with General Practice because you'd had enough hypertensive middle-aged men eating too many burgers and fat wives who swore they only ate lettuce. I carried the can while you did your Ph.D. Admittedly, you were great with the children until they went to school."

"And now?"

Claire decided she didn't like how Dave looked—like a man who'd kept too much in. Her hands. That wedding ring. If she was right, she'd be forty-nine by now. What options did she have? Maybe Dave was all there was, from here to eternity.

"So who am I now, Dave? I mean, who did I become?"

Dave smiled and raised his eyes to the fluorescent strip-lights on the ceiling. Lights cloaked with opaque plastic covers. Claire looked up at the lights—the blurry glow. She felt like those lights. Blurry but glowing. He sat down on the bed and took her hand.

"Now you are widely respected. An authority with clinical experience and academic rigour has brought you renown. Meanwhile, I'm still sticking a gloved finger up men's assholes to check for prostate cancer."

"Oh. Anything else?"

"We live in a beautiful Cape Cod-style house on a big lot. Nine years left on the mortgage. All our loans are paid off, college funds in good shape." Dave's features softened a little. "Mike and Jane are good kids. Fourteen and eleven. And your mother adores them, of course. Looks after them if you're here teaching and I'm on shift at the practice."

Claire reached out and took Dave's other hand, feeling the rough skin that once was soft and gentle. He was sweet. Maybe that was what she'd seen in him. Other than the usual things you felt when you were young. The hormone stuff. She looked into his eyes as they flitted anxiously here and there.

"And what about your parents?" she asked.

"Dad had a minor stroke two years ago, but he's OK. My Mum is about the same as yours. Getting by."

Claire leaned back on her pillows, removing her right hand from Dave's. She picked up the mirror again, her left hand still resting gently on Dave's palm. She examined her lined, drawn features.

"What happened to us, Dave?"

"We grew up is what happened. We got happy."

"Are you happy, Dave? Happy with me? Happy with life?"

"We've had our moments. Let's put it that way," Dave answered, standing up. He paused and looked up at the ceiling. "This is weird. I mean, if the research team expected anything, then it would have been a change in attitude, back to the beautiful soul you used to be. But all it's done is wipe out every memory you had since college."

Dave put his hand to his mouth as if to stop himself. The anguish in his face—this man who had been so carefree, so sure life would bring him what he wanted. Now he looked like what he was: a stressed daddy stuck in a job he didn't like, plagued by bills and demands on his time.

Claire, on the other hand, felt brand new. Only she didn't look it. She peered at her fading roots and wrinkled mouth in the mirror as if they belonged to someone else. Her wedding ring seemed a curiosity, like finding an old ticket stub in a coat pocket. Everything in her longed to get on with life, but most of it was behind her now, biologically at least. She grasped Dave's hand.

"Dave? Do you still want me?"

Dave's eyes shone with tears.

"It isn't that. It's…"

"It's what?"

She sat up in bed, feeling the gentle tug of an IV in her arm—saline, as she'd suspected, for hydration. She teased the line out of her arm and enveloped him in a hug. As she held him, she felt his body release, sobs heaving through his skinny frame. The Dave she remembered had been lean, powerful; now he'd hardened on the inside.

This wasn't her Dave. The old Dave who got reprimanded for asking a patient who'd stuck an electric toothbrush up their ass whether they wanted the batteries changed. This guy was a scarecrow, a pale shadow of the man she'd known when young.

She remembered wondering what her "adult life" would be like during her senior year, willfully ignoring that she was already three years into adulthood then. What was it John Lennon sang? "Life is what happens when you're busy making other plans." It was like she'd had her life—and now she got to rewind the tape and start again. Only she'd been put away in the wrong cassette box.

Dave pulled away from her and dried his eyes. Then he stood up, staring at her.

"Do you have any idea how much I hate General Practice? The freaks who present with Stage IIIB tumours only after exhausting every homeopathic and Christ-knows-what-pathetic cure. Diabetic executives who "can't" stop eating cookies. Claire, I did it all for you. I did it so you could get your Ph.D. I did it so you could become who you are."

Who knew idealistic Dave would become such a whiner? He was like a ship in a bottle with broken sails—interesting to look at but of no use.

"There was another reason I wanted you to do this, this thing," Dave continued. "I mean, apart from the fact you wanted to."

"What?"

Dave looked away again. He sighed, then words fell out of him like clothes from an overstuffed drawer:

"I wanted to rediscover the woman I'd loved. To dig out the beautiful, innocent person I'd married. Not the ball-breaking career woman you became. The Academic Director who was going to the top, no matter what."

Claire bit her lip. He sounded no happier with her than she was with him, not that she could remember. She was just judging by the anxious, bitter person standing before her.

She remembered that beach house on the Jersey Shore they'd borrowed in '97, waking early to hear the surf, Dave's sunburned body beside her on the cotton sheets. They'd been in love then. But now?

Now she barely recognized the man she'd go home with when she got out of here. Go to bed with. And those children she couldn't remember would be here soon—children who were just an aspiration for the student she used to be. But now she'd become a student again—kind of. A young woman in a middle-aged body.

She slid off the bed and put her arms around Dave.

"That nightmare career woman is long gone, Dr. Richards. And I have good news," she whispered in a low voice, lips grazing the wrinkled skin on his neck. "I'm better than ever. You'll see."

*

Four weeks later, she was back at work—trawling hospital wards and listening to the recommendations of housemen, nodding sagely and agreeing with everything they said. The terms she remembered, the science she knew; but the interest that had driven her professional life had vanished.

As with her clinical work, so with teaching: on her return to the office, she glanced through her lecture notes and slides with almo st supernal boredom—the impact of glycogen oxidation on long and short-term memory used to be her passion. But now she could barely keep her eyes on the page. She was obsessed with the future. A future she knew did not exist as she entered the final stages in her life. Despite her aging body, her heart and soul yearned for what might happen next. Every day, her mind twisted between her real life—Dave, her children; their house, her job—and dreams that would never be. She carried on her daily routine, listening, advising, lecturing and speaking. Attending faculty meetings and ferrying the kids around. And then she met Angelos.

Angelos was one of her post-graduate students working on the relationship between brain calcification in aging and memory loss. How we remember less the more decrepit we become. He'd come from Greece on a scholarship and had long dark hair that tumbled to his shoulders, deep brown eyes and a ready smile.

Claire could tell the females in the study group all wanted him—and she did too. Not so much for the physical stuff, that want had dulled—but for what he meant to her. For Claire, Angelos was freedom. Possibility. Escape.

*

"Professor Hetman? Are you OK?"

Claire awoke to find herself surrounded by students, Angelos on one knee before her, his brown eyes and three-day stubble captivating her.

"Is there anything we can do? Should we call someone?"

Angelos was looking at her. It was a Thursday a couple of weeks later. They'd come to the end of another discussion group, agreeing they had sufficient evidence to publish. She'd watched the students gather their stuff together—then blanked out. The other students crowded around her in a ring behind Angelos, clutching their laptops and notepad computers. Claire remembered using paper and pens in her day.

"I—I should be fine. Could someone call my husband? He's picking up the kids this afternoon."

*

When Dave came to pick her up, all she could think about was Angelos. As Dave stopped at a four-way intersection, she thought about the colour of Angelos' eyes. The purity of his skin, the taut body under his sweater.

Dave stared straight ahead, not speaking to her. They had barely touched each other since she'd hugged him in the recovery room, and God only knew how long it had been since they had made love. Or even said a kind word to each other.

"Jane got a good result in her spelling test," Dave said, still staring at the road.

"That's nice," Claire replied. Then she imagined holding Angelos, kissing him and thought about his body moving across hers.

"Tell me if you want me to defrost something for dinner. It's your turn to cook, but if you're feeling too tired, I'll take care of it."

Claire looked across at Dave's tensed lips. She touched him on his right forearm, his hand clutching the gear lever in their clapped-out Volvo station wagon.

"Dave."

"What is it?"

"Oh, nothing," she replied airily. "You just feel like a ball of pent-up anger these days."

"Well? Wouldn't you be? If you were married to you, I mean."

Claire leaned over and tugged at the steering wheel. Dave braked hard and skewed the car over to the hard shoulder.

"Claire! What the fuck?"

The tears finally came, falling thick down Claire's cheeks.

"Would I be pissed off at being married to me? Would I... fuck. I'd try to mix it up a little, not debating meatloaf versus pasta for dinner. Dave! We're a pair of fucking time bombs! How long before you try to kill me?"

"Claire—I would never—oh, fuck you."

Dave leapt from the car, slammed the door and walked fast up the highway. Claire scooched into the driver's seat, turned the ignition, slipped the ancient wagon into first, then shot off past Dave down the highway to their home six miles away.

She didn't call Dave's cell that night, and he didn't try to call her. She told the kids daddy was out for a beer with an old friend. And when Dave got home after midnight, it was clear he'd been drinking. Hard.

After she'd heard the toilet flush and Dave pad over to the spare room, she lay in bed and waited. When she thought he was asleep, she watched him sleeping on his back, his face half-lit by the moon. He seemed more at peace than the man she had known all those years ago.

The next morning, she woke up to find Dave had already had breakfast and was out walking the dog. She packed the kids off to school and headed out to work. On her way down their tree-lined street, Claire saw Dave and Bunny the Spaniel coming back. As she passed him in the vehicle, she didn't acknowledge him—nor did he pay her any attention. She put her foot down and raced the car to the stop sign at the end of their street.

Crossing the medical faculty plaza after parking, she spotted Angelos on a bench outside the teaching rooms. He was holding hands and kissing the neck of another student from her class, a slim blonde called Tiffany or something.

"Hey, Professor Hetman! Nice to see you back. Are you feeling better?"

Claire smiled, waved and said she was fine. She grabbed a coffee and headed for her office. But when she got there, she felt dizzy again. She hoped she wouldn't have another fit. She looked out the window and noticed it had started to rain small spots against the glass. It was that treatment. That potion. Whatever they had done to her, it was ruining—had ruined—her mind.

She went back downstairs, asked reception to tell people she was still sick and sent a terse email cancelling her classes for the day. She got in the beat-up Volvo and drove where she didn't know. After half an hour, she got to the coast and rolled along aimlessly, looking through the windscreen at the beach grasses and reeds, the way the wind threw the sand this way and that.

Eventually she came to an isolated house much like the one she had slept in with Dave when they were young. The clouds were thicker now, darker. The rain was growing more insistent. She stopped the car and got out, climbing to the top of the dunes that gave way to a flat expanse of beach studded with tidal pools and bits of driftwood. Then her eye was drawn to the horizon. That endless place between the grey-blue sea and the grey-black sky, the non-existent place where anything could happen and everything was possible. And she cried again, wondering if there were tears enough in the world to speak of the things she felt.

J.W. Wood is the author of five books of poems, a novel, and the forthcoming novella, *By Any Other Name* (Terror House Press, 2022). The recipient of awards from the BC Arts Council and the Canada Council for the Arts, his work has appeared widely in literary magazines worldwide, including *The Fiddlehead* (Canada), *AGNI* (US), *The Times Literary Supplement* (UK) and many others. A dual citizen of the UK and Canada, he presently divides his time between the two countries. jwwoodwriter.net

Analog

by Jessica Lee McMillan

fast-forward is a mode of a midlife crisis,
                I—then the obsolescent mechanic
—pay penance in time-bittered chain oil
—yellowed plastic buttons do not delete
the dawn   of immersive reality

my steel stamps strike page—keys
        wired to circuit brain slice air, thick
with transmission from wearable spacetime
            in the age of digital reproduction
hands phantom
for some reel-in—they soil pages in defence
with disappearance-wrought imprints
                    in clunky dub script

fallibly physical
—I am rattle of punched text bleeding
font to convex page—an analog shield
            —my dusty head strains to read
magnetic tape for vibration—I age—
                a laser scanning tracks
for someplace   to beat

Barefoot Grammar

by Jessica Lee McMillan

from urban deep to the city periphery
my feet picked up stray words,
road-metalled and callused,
adding to the lexical load

pavement shockwaves swam my pace
so I needed a tumble, needed a think,
washed through languages
in octopus roads

old soles welcomed new ground
hit the grass with a kiss
of pedestrian revelation
and grammar with soul

bare feet make gentler roads
and pave moss phonemes,
make trampolines of squares
and phrases of stepping stones

in lush bladed verbiage, over fences,
babbling feet, out of the stone flow
through stiles and alley and green lane,
internal weight rolls into the landscape

The Scabs, The Heat

by Jessica Lee McMillan

The ebb of summer warmed
the colding of age to an extent

Now when you bleed, you expect
gentleness from elements

Hungover, beg for rain on hot days;
life is a full-bellied escape

from grating surfaces; nothing
will let you go lightly

You cannot yield, only silks
and emperor's clothes raw the knees

You cannot feel and recoil
pre-emptively

With the scabs, the heat,
your road-rash body awaits your thanks

Jessica Lee McMillan is a poet, educator and civil servant. She has an English MA and is enrolled in the SFU Writer's Studio for 2022–2023. Her work has appeared in dozens of journals and literary magazines across Canada and the US, including *Train Poetry Journal*, *Pinhole Poetry*, *GAP RIOT Press*, *Antilang*, *Blank Spaces*, *Red Alder Review*, *SORTES*, *Lover's Eye Press*, Tiny *Spoon* and others. See more about her work on jessicaleemcmillan.com.

Offworlder Medical Issues

by Roxanne Barbour

Martians studying anatomy
Centaurans agreeing
humans
not belonging to
solar system standards

humans studying Martians
facial acne?
concerning
changing antibiotics
releasing stress inhibitors

skin sluicing off
Martian agony
help
humans welcomed
discovering infectious basis

Roxanne Barbour is a writer from Burnaby, BC, Canada. She started writing after she took early retirement in 2010. Roxanne has written and published numerous novels: *An Alien Collective*, *Revolutions*, *Sacred Trust*, *Kaiku*, *Alien Innkeeper*, *An Alien Confluence*, and *Alien Innkeeper on Particle*.

She also writes speculative poetry, and has had poems published in *Scifaikuest*, *Star*Line*, *Polar Borealis*, *Polar Starlight*, *Dwarf Stars*, and many other magazines.

No Strings

by Mitchell Toews

Part One: Synod

My name is Syn, short for Synod. Growing up on the Can-Cal Mainland Coast, across the Salish Sea at the top of Chief Dan George Island, I was raised for the most part by an electronic being endowed with a bank of Artificial Intelligence modalities that gave her a human character. I say "her" intentionally and in the traditional sense.

She was my Nana and this is her story.

My mother and father, Jason and Jessica Wannamaker, were successful and high-ranking computer design officers in the People's Science Army. I was a PSA brat, and a twelve-year-old abuser and eventual exasperator of a long string of come-and-go nannies employed by my busy parents. Drill sergeant or cuddly laissez-faire, I chewed them up and spat them out with my little tic-tac teeth like spent pumpkin seeds. My harried-but-dutiful parents tried every combination: a retired Spaceforce pilot with yellow hair growing out of his elephantine ears… the teenage rebel babysitter with implanted mini boar-tusks curling out of her lower jaw… even a sinewy 112-year-old Eurasian gymnast, her tattoo-rimmed eyes flashing hatred. None of them could handle my hellion ways. I knew every trick and made our home in the reforested hills north of Sullivan Bay a place of detention for my would-be overseers.

Our place was high above Grappler Sound and the Kwakiutl Speed Ferry rifled by each day, leaving a phosphorescent wake behind its hydrofoil masts. My parents, eyes clear and ready for duty, boarded the Speed Ferry tender the second Monday of each month and returned dog-tired and slump-shouldered on the successive last Saturday.

After I sent a pair of Easter Island exchange students packing, their cheap radiation vests clacking as they ran for their HovUber, my parents came up with a new plan.

"Electronic Nannies. We design them, we build them, we upgrade them, we assess them. After Soldier-Security, Nannies are the PSA's biggest category! In this sense, we owe our livelihood, our water ration, our radiation shielding quotas—everything, really—to them," Dad said.

Mom tilted her head. "So…why don't we *employ* one of them?"

"Exactly. Exacta-Mondo. *'Oba kratjcht jo!'* as Syn's namesake, Great Uncle Synod from Manitoba, was prone to say."

Dad loved the old language—called Trader Lingo, or TL—especially since it had undergone a resurgence in recent years. It was considered *chic,* or as one would say in TL, *seea fine!* The lingo was especially popular with the upscale science set like my parents.

"Syn… listen, buddy, how'd ya like to have a PSA Nanny?"

Of course, I was familiar with these things. As far as I knew, they were awkward, slow-moving, simple-minded gatekeepers. A hybridized ambulatory protein generator station/medico/soccer mom occupying a mid-level rung in the human-electro-animal status hierarchy, above a trained animal-clone bodyguard, but below an average citizen.

"I thought you weren't allowed to have one… 'cause, conflict of interest?"

"I made Intentionalizer Status last month," Mom said. "With great responsibility comes great perks."

"Gotcha," I replied.

"So, what-ya-say?" Dad asked, then repeated the question in TL, "*Waut saje dü?*"

I shrugged, did a military toe-pivot and sauntered upstairs. I wondered how it might be to have a PSA Nanny around. One loaded up with all of the best modalities: Deconfrontation AI, Conversation AI, Adolescent Games, Riddles, and Fart Jokes AI…

"Best thing is," Dad called after me, "I'm up for an Intentionalizer promotion too and then Mom and I could pre-load our Nanny with as many modality ports as we wanted. All of them! She'd have the capacity for virtually unlimited upgrades. Indefinitely."

"Hmm…"

"That means that at some point, your Nanny would have, essentially, a synthetic human brain. Probably one of the first. She'll be top grade. What do you think?"

"Yeah." That would be *seea fine*… "By the way… she?"

"Busted," my mom said. "Well, you know, the appearance features are enhanceable and—just for fun—I've picked some physical traits from my family. Great-times-seven Oma Helen."

"She's the one in that picture on the piano, right?"

"Yep," they answered simultaneously.

"Give you my answer by nineteen-hundred," I said.

Part Two: Nana

The Kwakiutl Speed Ferry slowed. Then came to a complete halt, bobbing gently in the quiet waters of the Sound. I watched from my room as the vessel stood-to off our jetty. An eight-prop drone with jet-assist took off from the foredeck above the cargo hold with a coffin-sized box dangling vertically below it. The propwash drew a dark blue trail across the surface of the water, and the craft's warning claxon sounded impatient as it hovered above the concrete deck of our community dock. The crate, marked in bold letters, "*PSA,*" descended smoothly.

"Detach, detach, detach!" the speaker blared. Then the machine swooped away in reverse, the loose cable reeling up into the underbelly as it sped back to the ferry boat. I could feel the afternoon breeze starting up as I ran down the path towards the shore, my eyes glued on the crate. The wind piped up as I ran onto the deck and our jetty caretaker met me at the box.

"Gettin' breezy," he said, putting a gloved hand against the side of the upright crate and testing it for balance. "Oh, man. Heavy. No fear of the wind toppling that!" He spoke into his communication mic, "Bernice, this is Art. Do you have a minute to buzz yer loading spider over to the Wannamakers' and hump a crate up to their place?"

He listened to her reply, the wind whipping his longish, grey hair. "Lessee, says…155 kg…it's about two metres…yep, lotsa grapple hooks—it's an easy lift for your rig. You got the 750, eh? That thing's a brute."

He paused and felt in his pocket. Withdrawing two miniature bananas he held them out to me. "Oatmeal or pear flavour?"

Pear was my favourite. As Art separated the two small synthetic fruit pieces, a slight whirring sound emitted from a diamond grid of speaker holes drilled into the box at head height.

"Greetings, earthlings!" chirped the box, with what sounded like a giggle. "My review of the individual—Wannamaker, Synod—indicates full capacity: 22% carbohydrate, 44% fat, and 34% protein. The minana will add an unneeded 24 kcal of carbohydrate. It'll make you sluggish, Syn. I know it's delicious, but it'll spike your blood sugar."

Send this Nanny back, I thought, twisting my face into a scowl.

"You are what you eat," Art said, slowly withdrawing the minana.

Just then, Bernice arrived in her bright red spider. "You want me to hoist this piece of *schiet* up to the Wannamaker place?" she shouted to Art. Seconds later, the female voice came from the crate. Bilingually, in smoothly-accented TL and skookum CanCal English, the voice said, "*Nijch soo prost, Mejal*—ease up on the potty-mouth, girl!"

Art was about to answer Bernice's question, when once again, the holes in the crate spoke. "Bernice! How good of you to arrive here so promptly. If I may, could I please request that Synod read the release phrase printed on the box immediately below the audio perforations? Syn must read it aloud to actuate me."

There ain't no strings on me, was printed in black font.

"Who's in there?" Bernice asked, nodding her chin at the crate and reaching down to grab a dangling minana from Art.

"I am Nanny Lena, the Wannamakers' new household AI unit. I'm here to run the Wannamaker house. *Etj sie dee Bauss!*"

There was a stunned silence. "Tabernac on toast!" Bernice said, slowly chewing her minana.

"I'll second that," Art offered, adding, "She speaks Trader... says she's the boss, but can she climb the rocky path up t' Wannamaker's, is my question."

"Once young Synod actuates me, I'll be in full ambulatory mode. I will disengage myself from my compostable transfercrate and carry it with me up to the house. I am fully rigged for steep and irregular ascent and descent and even have the latest auto-deploy micro prop assist widgets, so I can hover with a load of 72 kg, in a wind of up to 50 kph," she explained.

Intrigued, I spoke loud and slow, "There ain't no strings on me." The crate began to hum and vibrate. Bolts reversed themselves out of their threaded bondage, and the door swung open.

"Gangway for Nanny Lena," the robot said merrily, exiting the transfer case as Bernice, Art, and I looked on.

"She's the latest and greatest, that's fer damn sure," Art ventured, pocketing his remaining minana.

"Art! Language!" Nanny Lena said with a wink at me.

With that, she spun around at the waist to face Bernice,

"Thank you so much for your attendance, Bernie, but as you can see, I am not in need of assistance. Also, I have determined that your Loading Spider is past its warranty period and requires a scheduled maintenance session. Shall I arrange that for you, or would you prefer to handle it yourself?"

Bernice's jaw hung slack, looking past Nanny Lena to Art. "This is the damnedest gadget yet! Homely too. Those PSA folks are gonna turn us all into bojack robots, next thing you know," she said.

Before Bernice could say any more, Nanny Lena spoke again, over her shoulder, "Also, congratulations on your pregnancy! I'm sure Sergeant Loewen will make an excellent father!"

"But, I'm not..." Bernice began in protest, then stopped, a puzzled look on her face.

"Guess again, Bernie, *you slut.*" It was the Nanny's purring voice, meant for me alone, clear in my communication earpiece.

Nanny Lena looked down at me and placed a Cowichan-sweater-sleeved arm around my shoulders. We left together, the cumbersome crate hefted up on the shoulder of the pert, trim 1.5 metre frame of my new, undisputed *Bauss.*

Part Three: Onset

Twenty-nine years. Hundreds of automatic upgrades for Lena, or as I called her almost since the day she arrived, "Nana." For me, there had been a wife, a divorce, two kids, three academic degrees, and a top job in the PSA. I took over Mom's role as the CanCal head of Security when she retired.

"The forecast calls for a squall to come in from the sea and hit the jetty at 14:14:07. Do you wish to reschedule the Hover-Wuver for the trip to Port Hardy?"

I poured milk into my cereal, then slid the container towards Nana to put away. "Reschedule my what?"

"Reschedule your HovUber. It should be on the jetty at 13:55… and by the way," she slid the milk back at me, "you could use the exercise." She patted her midriff.

Her sense of humour, always at the ready and often filled with ancient or arcane references that I had stopped trying to place years ago, was likely the cause for the "HoverWuver" mix-up. Her massively updated AI mind was essentially incapable of a raw mistake, although the occasional malfunction of vocal or auditory hardware could cause apparent errors.

She smiled. "'HoverWuver'… the name of a Third World War fighter-class hoverbot that served in the Fifth Battle of Ukraine. Shall I look for a memory-enhancing vitamix for you, Syn?"

"Nice cover, Nana, my dear, but I think you have a loose…"

"Circuit? Screw? How passé! That's impossible," she interrupted with an electric sniff and left the room with a hum. "It's like you're against me lately, Syn!"

*

Next week, it happened again. We had been arguing for at least ten minutes even though since age sixteen or so, I had essentially given up arguing with Nana. What was the point? She had access to, and perfect recall of, limitless factual resources. But her responses had developed an almost human tone and recently had taken on an authentic, human-like angry feel.

Nana and I had a wealth of mutual experience. We had grown up under one another's ever-watchful eyes. We had each evolved. Nanny Lena went from a simple matron to becoming my most constant companion and simultaneously my "Nana" and best friend. We both grew and learned via education, experimentation, travel, and maturity. Lena also grew via automatic upgrade. The net result was that I loved her in a way reserved for those who care enough to be frank, who love deeply enough to risk our wrath and tell us what we need to hear, not what we want.

"There's no point in arguing," I said for the third time. "The sauce bottle was in the oven. Still is. I found it when I was going to warm up some hot wings. It was there, on the rack, label facing forward in the precise centre of the space—exactly the way you would place it."

"Fiddlesticks! *Kuh schiet!* I am incapable of putting hot sauce in any place except the third row of the left refrigerator door, near the anterior side. Mustards to the posterior, sauces to the front, and syrups next row down. I created the org chart and have followed it for umpteen years…"

"See! There! *Umpteen.* That is imprecise and a vernacular not common to twenty-second-century CanCal English or Trader Lingo, the languages used in our household. Why would you use such an obtuse phrase, Nana? And why did you put the sauce in the oven? Was it a joke? 'Hot' sauce, so you put it in a hot place?"

"Twenty-nine years, four months and 18 days is an umpteenth's-worth. Particularly when dealing with an unfailingly obstinate and intractable sort of person like you. Also, as a humourist, you are a damned mule-skinner, or *Shinde,* if you prefer Trader Lingo."

"My, my, Nana…out-of-bounds dialect, frequent adverb use—remember what you always taught me…"

"*Oba jo.* Frequent use of adverbs indicates that your verbs are weak or inaccurate."

"Exactly right…" I replied.

"There. You just proved my point."

I succumbed. Nana flashed me a too-human glare and turned to leave the kitchen. As she passed the oven, she paused, then halted suddenly. She opened the door, snatched the hot sauce bottle from its perch, and swung open the fridge. Without looking at me, she hummed tonelessly and murmured, "This is very strange," and placed the bottle in its designated spot.

I watched her depart. "It's nothing," I said to myself. I whispered a translation of the old Trader Lingo rhyme as a further calming tonic: "*Enn Droon ess en Droch,*" I began, upon which Nana stopped and whispered back via communicator, "A dream is as naught…"

"*Emm Hamd ess en Loch,*"

"A shirt has a spot…"

"*Wea jistre ess, ess uck noch.*"

"Was there before, like as not."

Part Four: The Farewell Lexicon

The SeaVan hospital was one of the new, in-vogue retro buildings. The art-deco structure was outfitted with a multitude of cultural influences inside to represent the many peoples and Nations resident in CanCal. Hospitals were no longer necessary except for severe accidents, violent crime, and the few lingering late-life afflictions that still plagued the human species. Ambulances could handle almost everything else, at the scene or via in-home visitation. Hospitals had evolved to serve as dignified and pleasant final off-ramps for the dying. People typically enjoyed their later years—the "Roaring 120s"—in the company of pets and old friends, some real, some holographic, some AI clones. The staff of extreme empaths made the transition from life to death one of comfort and peace.

I felt weak. A sense of surreal surrender was my state of mind. This place, as pretty and comforting as it was and designed as if drawn directly from my memories, was no comfort for me today. No comfort at all.

"Well, there's nothing in the rules against it," Doctor Lhálhewels said. She was an older person herself, perhaps in her nineties, who sat in a low chair while the rest of us reclined on soft cedar mats spread over the floor. The doctor re-crossed her legs and leaned forward, tugging at the hem of her skirt. She wore eye glasses and makeup in the style of the 1940s and I found it pleasing. "Certainly, every individual, especially you, considering your rare status as a second-gen Intentionalizer, is welcome in this facility."

"Great. Where do I sign?" I said, leaning forward a bit myself.

She smiled but in a way that, despite her empath skills, conveyed more a sense of unease than of agreement.

"Yes. We'll get to that I'm sure, but I just don't have the right paperwork available at this time. I'm sorry. I'm certain we can operationalize it, but it is an uncommon request. First of its kind, actually. Can you bear with me while I dig up the correct individual at Hospice Care and file a custom request? We're a bit draconian here in our rules and regs. It's part of the whole retro look and feel. Paper forms, filing cabinets, colour-coded microfiche…whatever that is…or was. Even I don't remember…"

Beside me, Nana sat prim and straight-backed in her chair. She had returned from the washroom. Her clothes, hair, and make-up had been expertly rearranged to match those of Doctor Lhálhewels'. She looked like Greer Garson, and I would not have blinked if she had lit a cigarette and removed a fleck of tobacco from her lips with a demure, white-gloved hand. My mom and dad, settled in their own hospice space in Windsor, were at a 1968 Tigers ballgame reenactment—part of their enriched experience—and they had promised to HovUber out for tomorrow morning. Tomorrow was Nana's official day of admittance here in VanSeattle.

When the doctor returned, she held a sheaf of papers. She motioned me to bring my chair to her desk and be seated.

"Here we are! Thanks for waiting. Nanny Lena, are you comfortable? May we get you anything before Syn and I complete this paperwork?"

"Call me Nana, and… I'd like a gin martini. Make it, uhh, dry," Nana replied, wetting the spiral of a kiss-curl on her forehead with moistened fingertips.

"She's joking," I said to Doctor Lhálhewels in a soft voice, a whisper, really, though this was no use. Nana could hear whatever I said through our communicators. I glanced at Nana, and she grinned at me, pretending to puff on a cigarette and blow smoke.

"Birthdate?"

I knew they had all of this information, but this too was part of the hospice immersion experience. I felt as though the doctor was required to follow these protocols. Nana seemed to be enjoying it anyway, so I played along. "2090, June 15."

The interview lasted twenty minutes. I was distracted and flushed by the end of it. The finality was making me queasy and I wished I had a THD relaxation ampule.

"There," the doctor stacked the papers with a noisy shuffling motion on the oak desk. Propping her eyeglasses on her forehead, she rose and held her hand out to shake, which I did. "That's everything. Tomorrow morning, any time after 9:00 will be fine. The Wannamaker suite of rooms will be properly prepped as per your earlier instructions… ready for Nana. I look forward to meeting your parents then. It's a big day, and I want everything to be perfect."

*

We had taken a private HovUber, and it waited for us just outside of the imposing stone stairway at the hospice's grand entrance. Nana stepped cautiously, although this was all part of the retro play-acting. In reality, she could have done back-flips down the steps and finished with a two-handed dunk at the bottom. Physically, she was still as strong and lithe as the day she arrived on our jetty.

"So. Are you excited for tomorrow? All your dreams come true?" Nana said.

"Anything but," I said, my chin on my chest as I slouched in the Uber.

"Why? These hospices are renowned for their care and attention to detail. There's nothing you'll want, Syn, no matter what!"

I stared at her for a long time. I began to hum a song Nana used to enjoy singing to me when I was a child. It was a beautiful old folk ballad and she could sing it perfectly. In three-part harmony, her voice split into a wavering trio—exquisite and fine as antique silk.

We sang together, her adding instruments and arranging the piece as if we were in a New York recording studio. After a while, she quieted and a soft look filled her eyes. The rough water of the Salish Sea flashed beneath us and ranks of waves poured out of the west like an advancing army, infinite and unyielding.

I thought of the last months. Nana's frequent miscues. Her attention to the weather, cooking and local news; all topics safe and mundane had become her stock in trade. No more of the complicated but always on-point references and puns. Her characteristic spontaneous and often acerbic one-liners had disappeared. Repetition, a certain dullness—though still vastly superior to all but the sharpest Mensa human—was evident to me.

Through the mounting evidence, my mother was adamant in her refusal to believe it. "She is, despite her wonderful, almost uncanny human caricature, still an artificial being. A creation of science, not an—not an *act of God*. Nana's soul, such as we understand it, does not, and cannot, exist," my mother said. "She is not organic. Sure, her mind is 'human' in many ways, but still is chemical and electronic and magnetic."

I heard my mother's words, my appreciation underscored by our mutual expertise. Mom and I were, after all, among the world's top foremost experts on AI. Still, though, I was convinced. Plus, I had retrieved all of the update logs. Nana had received over 700 downloads. In effect, the PSA had synthesized a human brain inside of Nana's head.

This conclusion fits all of the evidence. Nana's symptoms were too clinically exact, too damning in their timing and severity. I knew Nana too well to disregard or dispute the obvious, tragic prognosis. Immutable facts or not, Mary Shelley or not—Nana had Alzheimer's disease. She was entering the later stages of her ability to continue to disguise her illness and fake competence. The progression was well-known and varied little from patient to patient. Nana was Stage Four, or perhaps early Five. Even with the assistance of artificial intelligence to find a cure, we have been unable to do so and now—now this, I thought...

Nana, arguably the owner of the most human-like brain of any AI in existence, contracted Alzheimer's disease. This is a fate no one foresaw. So ironic. So cruel...

Beyond the full understanding and logic of science, and similar to the catastrophic novel coronavirus of 2020, that went from bat to human, Alzheimer's disease had jumped from human to AI.

With AI pragmatism, Nana had refused all attempts to do the mechanical examination required to reveal her exact condition. Instead, she made an eloquent plea for death with dignity, which was granted. The hospice had specific, legal instructions for her care. In the end, my parents, as the "legal owners," were granted agency for this decision. They asked my advice, and I said, we must simply follow Nana's wishes without hesitation or variation.

She chose death or at least the AI version of that finality. But because of the circular viciousness of the disease, she now had trouble clearly recalling this choice or the events that followed her decision.

We rode together in silence. The hum of the HovUber's reactor lulled me to sleep. When I awoke, I found her holding my hand.

"I used to do this when I first came to care for you and your parents. I'd feed you, and we'd do some activity, boating or hiking. Then you'd tire out, and I'd sing to you or read to you. *The Best Thing Since Sliced Bread*, *The Prince and the Pauper*. It wasn't long before I thought of you as my own, and I always believed you had similar thoughts towards me."

"I did, from almost the first day. And by the way, you still sing beautifully. You remember all the words—I don't."

Nana nodded. "So, tell me, Syn… what has happened to me? You *are* Syn, yes? I'm sure you are, though I can't place you just now." She smiled and looked away before continuing, her eyes on the coastal mountains. "I can recall a boy named Syn. Not you maybe, or maybe you are… but you look like someone nice, anyway. I know something is strange these days. I feel it, but for some reason I can't reconcile it, mathematically. Logically, like I normally would. Do you know what's happening? If you tell me from the beginning and explain how it all is… do I have a degenerative issue? Chemical? Mechanical? Have you run a diagnostic? My memory banks seem disorganized. Am I broken?"

She paused to regroup. I recognized the shift and the short hitch at the onset of a pre-recorded program—she had switched over to something that she had set for auto-replay some day in the future, based on a specific combination of circumstances. Today was that day.

"Hello. To overcome my abnormal condition in the short term, I've set a repair program up to patch my memory almost instantly when a piece goes missing from what you tell me now. This way, for a few minutes at least, I'll be able to understand the situation. Explain what is happening to me clearly and simply and in one telling. I'll comprehend, long enough for us to be clear on it, together. For a little while, at least. My condition appears to be terminal and I can't stop my comprehension from going away at some point, but maybe that's alright." She nodded again after the speech and fixed me with a searching, confused gaze from which I could not look away.

And so I went through it, step by step. At the end, Nana stared straight ahead. She did not speak, but was calm. She did not move for a few minutes. My sense of her was overpoweringly one of relief, as if a difficult task had been completed and now the path was clear to take on the next thing.

"So, Nana, tomorrow, it's not me who will stay at the hospice…"

"Where we were earlier today, right? A nice place." She smiled bravely; the computer patch she had installed in her circuitry gave her this answer but the Alzheimer's was eroding it and shrouding it almost as quickly.

"Yes. It's you, remember. You are the one to stay at the hospice. It took a lot to get them to agree to take you. You are the first. The first AI, Nana, to be admitted for hospice care. Also, the first AI with Alzheimer's to be admitted."

She looked down, and her hands moved expressively as if she was coaxing a thought out. "I have a human disease?"

"Yes. You are the first."

She thought again, her hands rubbing together. Then she reached out to touch my forearm. "There are no… there are no strings on me," she said, her gaze drifting away towards the horizon. She held onto my arm and then asked, "And comes a time, not long after?"

"Yes. Comes a time when your power will be no more. When your processor will stop functioning, and then your systems will all… cease."

My words caught in my throat, and I looked away, seeing waves break on the open water below. Nana's voice was small and distant. She spoke beautifully in Trader Lingo, making the rough language seem like the most delicate and most ancient of poetry. I turned back to look into her eyes. They shone, backlit from the knowledge of her fate, a fate she clutched like something as dear and present as love or happiness or the feeling of kindness and of doing for others.

"*Fe de Doot es tjeen Krüt jewosse,*" she said in a hushed voice. Her hand rested softly on mine. "For death, there is no herb grown." The simple proverb was, it seemed in that quiet moment, like a truth that had finally come to rest. A journey's end, untroubled, natural, human.

Mitchell Toews is a writer, sometimes painter, gardener, avid windsurfer, and rower. Approximately 100 literary journals and anthologies have published Toews' fiction since 2016. The author is a three-time Pushcart Prize nominee and a finalist in several prose competitions including a highly valued shortlist for the 2022 J.F. Powers Prize for Short Fiction. Publication of a collection of short stories is forthcoming with Winnipeg's At Bay Press in 2023. Mitch recently completed a review of his debut novel, working as a protege to Canadian novelist, playwright, poet, and educator Armin Wiebe through a "Mentorship Microgrant" sponsored by the Writers' Union of Canada.

Food Diary

by Jessica Berry

Monday (1,000 Calories)
Food diary, I confess, I have been mulish. Today is a new week and a sacred time to
Slough off these flabby ropes tugging at my back. Correct the curmudgeonly cat scratchings
Reddening my stomach. I will not hog leather staffroom sofas like an army tank; I will be Notably angular and dream of a body to stretch or starve for.

Tuesday (800 Calories)
Instagram has been an excellent motivator. The artisanal inner sanctum drink £10
Tart smoothies, swear by beetroot brownies, rebrand thigh gaps as adages, kiss
Pectoral muscles and Balenciaga pool slippers, dot the i's in *paid promotion* with evanescent Hearts—I'll emulate their eloquent lines and dream of a body to lie for.

Wednesday (600 Calories)
Cruel infections sting in my sweet teeth: a serrated reminder of all the naughty things I've
Consumed before this new me. The spirits of masticated pizza, factory calamari, glazed

Cherries tough as knuckles rise to gums. I press a hot water bottle to
Contaminated cheeks and dream of a body to spit up sins for.

Thursday (400 Calories)
Today the garden is a greenhouse: I brave a swimsuit. It is no longer my right
To read romance novels on the back porch; swap these for screeds that teach
How to suppress appetites with cigarettes and black coffee. The neighbour's children
Use their trampoline; I run inside at their launch. I dream of a body that now I must hide for.

Friday (2,500 Calories)
Food diary, let me poke out my pupils with your accusatory edges. Palm tree print
Boiler suits have become my official *occasion* uniform. Sticky cages in the balmy air
Make it impossible to disassociate from this rejected bin liner of skin. I've
Imbibed too many salvers of warm wine. My dream body is detritus, stuck to the glass.

Saturday (4,000 Calories)
I can no longer stand the puissant stench of fake tans blending. It burns knots in my throat; it is a memento of the singer massacring Neil Diamond, too many tapas options, syrup sucked from cocktail straws, 24-hour chicken shop on Dublin Road of the mistakes. The open mouth pivots back to bidding a dream body goodbye.

Sunday (The Sabbath Forbids Counting)

The minister says, "this is your father's house." I wipe down the surface of my life with

Bleach. Smoothing his cream horn collar, he preaches of the palatial physique bestowed

Unto all who deny fleshy temptations, who get wristbands to Heaven. Food diary, I will

Pick up your fat spine again tomorrow. In tandem, we can dream of a body to die for.

Jessica Berry grew up beside the seaside of Bangor, County Down, Northern Ireland. She is an English teacher at the Belfast Model School for Girls. In 2021, Jessica was placed in Bangor's annual poetry contest hosted by the Aspects Literary Festival. Her work has also been included in publications such as *Drawn to the Light* and *A New Ulster*. She is working on her first poetry collection, inspired by Irish myths and fables.
Social media links: @jessicaruth.poetry on Instagram

Browbeating, Myself

by Susan Alexander

I had two once, each a soft brown caterpillar crawling away
from the other.
> My twin eye-muffs. My furry ledges.

They were unsatisfactory, I know.
Hair grew outside the outline permitted by fashion,
feathered towards the temples in a typical splay of indecision.
The unibrow tuft I eradicated weekly.
Salon butchers, how they loved to wax and rip.
> My shoe polish brushes. My feather boas.

Did they fall out when I was reproducing myself?
So sleep-deprived, I didn't look in the mirror for years?
Only the odd, wayward hair remains, an invisible few.
> My ocular roofs. My little bears.

It was when my best-friendship was teetering on friend-divorce
that her mother said to me *where are your eyebrows?*
I hadn't noticed they'd left. Did they migrate to my upper lip?
Were they irredeemably singed when the gas barbecue exploded?
> My teeny shoulders. My rainbows after tears.

Missing: two eyebrows, indifferent shape, sentimental value.
A reward for their return.

Now, in the time

of wrinkle and sag   should I get them

microbladed back?   Find a tattooist

to pierce and   tint perfect

bows over my   drooped lids?

And if the artist draws on two black slugs? I've seen it done.
And will they work, these faux definers? My personal and permanent *trompe l'oeil?*
Will they move up and down like nonverbal punctuators in
querulous shrugs?

Oh, hold off a little longer! Let my eyeglasses spoof
those most desirable arches! Or hide their lack under a fringe
(as they call it in Angleterre)! Thus do I ruminate while other
outlines blur and the clock ticks me towards the inevitable door.
Oh, my pine cones. My lost kittens.

Ode to My Thighs

by Susan Alexander

At sixteen, you high jumpers and long jumpers of sinew and lean
grew weighty and marbled as grain-fed beef. How I prayed
to wake up without your bulk, arise slenderly and shivering,
slide into tightest jeans and acceptable places like the tiny shrines
in boys' eyes. I lassoed you with measuring tape,
and counted every carb and fat. I kept you under wraps,
hid the harem of two under loose skirts and dark slacks.

And despite the shame and every magazine spread of skinny,
this is what they'd reach for in the dark, the lust-blind
with their groping-stroking pinches at all that's lush and pliable,
these finger-sinking tender parts, these pink pleasurers,
twin larders of feast, the whole Latin mass of you:

    O Maximus and Magnus
    Gracilis Sartorius
    Rectus Femoris

O hollowed narthex at the top! O bliss and nimbus!
You temple pillars soaring up towards the glory!

Susan Alexander is a poet and writer living in British Columbia on Nexwlélexm/Bowen Island, the traditional and unceded territory of the Squamish people. Susan's work has appeared in anthologies and literary magazines throughout Canada, the U.S. and the U.K. She is the author of two collections of poems, *Nothing You Can Carry*, 2020, and *The Dance Floor Tilts*, 2017, from Thistledown Press. Her suite of poems called *Vigil* won the 2019 Mitchell Prize for Faith and Poetry while some of her other work has received the Vancouver Writers Fest and Short Grain awards.

The Body of Work: An Essay on Andre Dubus II

by Eve Morton

I discovered Andre Dubus II's work after giving birth to my first child. My husband had a worn-down anthology of short fiction from his university days, and while my son slept, I picked it up and began to page through it. At the time, I had no idea I was searching for relief from the cloud of postpartum depression. But from the stories I read—"The Yellow Wallpaper" by Charlotte Perkins Gilman, ironically one of the many in this collection—I started to piece together what was fact, what was fiction, and feel my way out of the darkness.

Andre Dubus' "The Intruder" was one of the many stories in this collection. I'd never heard of him before. Despite my degree in English Literature, and studying the works of typically masculine fiction present in the road novel for my Ph.D (think Kerouac, Steinbeck, and more recently Michael Chabon). I had only ever come across the work of his son, Andre Dubus III. Even then, I still hadn't read much of him. After my son was born and I realized that my head wasn't quite right, I promised to myself that I'd still attend to things I loved before having a baby. Fiction had always been one of those things, and since I didn't feel like I had the wherewithal or the concentration to read a novel, short fiction it was.

I was immediately drawn to "The Intruder." The story begins with a boy's fantasy life, where he imagines soldiers on a battlefield, only to be forced back to reality at home, with his parents out for the evening. Soon, his sister invites her boyfriend over, a prospect that makes the boy uncomfortable to say the least. I won't spoil the story's eventual ending too much (though this is one of Dubus' most anthologized stories). But the boy's fascination with fantasy—and the ever present literal Chekov's gun in the story—leads to an interesting ending that moved me. Deeply. There was something so vulnerable, so frail about this young boy holding a gun and unable to differentiate fantasy from reality, stranger from familiar, and then the good from the bad. This deeply resonated with my own struggle at that time.

My postpartum depression came on suddenly. At the time, I believed it to be nothing but the baby blues, which happens to upwards of 85% of all women post-birth. I was prepared for the tears that I knew would come in the aftermath, from exhaustion, pain, and the profound lack of sleep. I didn't blink at the inability to sleep without crying. I sprang awake from extreme nightmares about people I loved dying. I didn't even get that concerned when I started to have intrusive thoughts about jumping in front of cars whenever I went outside for a walk. That was just exhaustion talking. It was the fact that my role had changed and part of me still resisted that change. Also, I had a really mean midwife. It seems so odd to say—don't people hate the coldness of their OBGYNs and feel exalted as a goddess incarnate by the midwives?—but it was true for me. My midwife browbeat me during my labour, telling me I wasn't trying hard enough and even admitting that she was being mean. According to her, "it got results." The doctor who eventually delivered my son (there was a minor complication the midwife could not handle), she was kind and considerate. Go figure.

All in all, I thought I was lucky. My pregnancy was near perfect, one of the happiest times of my life. Despite that rather strange experience with my warring medical professional, I thought I was doing fine in the aftermath. And because I had always assumed that postpartum depression came with either vivid hallucinations (à la "The Yellow Wallpaper"), thoughts of harming your child (which I, blissfully and thankfully, did not have), or stemmed from environmental conditions and a general lack of support from husband/family (I didn't have this at all; my husband was fantastic and so was his family), I shrugged it off. I toughed it out.

Then I read "The Intruder," which in many ways demonstrates the perils that come from toughing something out. When I read the biography that came with the story in the anthology, it mentioned how Andre Dubus, near the end of the 1980s, stopped to help two motorists who had run over an abandoned bike. In this process, he was hit by an oncoming vehicle. He managed to push one of the original people he wanted to help out of the way, saving her life. He did not manage to save the other person, and as for his own injuries, he would eventually lose the use of his legs, and spend the rest of his life in a wheelchair. He would continue to write from this chair—even penning several essays about it, collected in his *Meditations from a Moving Chair* and in *Broken Vessels*—but he would also continue to write short fiction. His last collection, *Dancing After Hours*, documents several people with injuries similar to his own.

In particular, one story is about a man who takes his attendant/nurse with him to the local bar. Everyone drinks, is happy, and talks about life and morality, as most people speak about such topics throughout Dubus' work. But the story is a keen observation into the human body's frailty, how one snap event can take so much from you physically, and then usher you into a new world that presents you with limitation after limitation, struggle after struggle. Despite wanting to on several occasions, you can't just give up. You must carry on. As the title indicates, you must keep dancing, even after hours.

So much of Dubus' ethos comes from his Catholicism. Dubus went to mass almost every day during some parts of his life, and he spoke reverently in his fiction and nonfiction about taking the communion. It can be easy to see his topics and his stories through the lens of religion only. Or, alternatively, only view them through his military career, since his first book was called *The Lieutenant*, based on some of his experiences as a marine, and these themes also appear in his short fiction. Dubus was very much a man of faith and honour in all the stereotypical ways, all the ways in which I can see criticism of his work crop up that focuses on the downside of this toxic masculinity, like his obsessive need to write about adultery, and to commit a lot of it himself (the horrible and dire consequences of some of those decisions are documented by his son, Andre Dubus III, in his memoir *Townie*).

But I can't let go of Dubus as a writer. I especially can't let go of his fiction. Be it that first story of "The Intruder," the last one in the *Dancing After Hours* collection, "Anna," "They Live in California," or any of the other stories written by him that I've read now. And continued to read as I went through treatment and recovery for my postpartum depression. They're just too important to me, and I think, important to anyone who has a body, or as Adrienne Rich puts it in her work, anyone who is "of woman born." Not everyone needs to be a mother, or a mother with postpartum depression, to appreciate the nuance of Dubus' writing—but I think everyone born should give him a chance. Merely because I have never seen anyone document the frailty of the body after a massive change so well and with such conviction that the difference after the fact is not bigger or worse. It just is. Even though he lost the use of his legs, Dubus writes in several essays how he would never regret stopping to help those motorists. Why would he? He did what he was supposed to do. And like him, I don't regret having my son, though for a while there, living with him next to me was like living in a nightmare landscape no one else could see.

My story has a happy ending; my husband and I realized what was happening. I spoke freely about how hard it was to keep up with daily life, how fearful I was and how I couldn't sleep, and I got help. This involved going on medication—something I strongly resisted at first—but they turned out to be a boon. I could enjoy my son again, enjoy my body again, and soon afterwards, we were pregnant again, with another boy, and happy to be that way. Yet the experience of that summer didn't just go away. A scar that lingered in my psyche, the nights that I was up crying and crying, literally tearing my hair out because I could think of nothing else to do. The screaming matches I had over nothing but bad jokes with my husband. Those items, those memories, will always linger.

And I see that lingering sense of lasting change in Dubus' fiction, the frailty of the body and mind together that can only be remedied through some kind of soul. I am not speaking of his Catholicism here, believe it or not, but the sexuality and physicality he expresses in his work. That kind of bodily authenticity is, perhaps, a consequence of his military service and his Catholicism, but manages to transcend those limitations at the same time.

Dubus was an avid runner for most of his life, only switching to conditioned walking a few years before his accident. Then he switched to swimming after losing his legs. He speaks eloquently about the use of his own body, his physicality, and the bodies of his characters in fiction that truly speaks of embodiment; something that I, up until reading Dubus, had only seen in the feminist writers of the 1970s and 1980s.

Dubus also speaks about sex—particularly, the kind of sex without birth control, the kind of sex that produces babies—with particular reverence. The amount of times he says 'womb' in his fiction is more than any author I have ever read, possibly including some of those feminist authors of the 1970s and 1980s. He talks about feeling a female character's womb as a man, and women feeling their wombs as mothers and lovers. He talks about the sensation of being inside someone, the sensation of someone being inside someone else and of a baby coming out of a mother. He talks about penises and vulvas and breasts and the mouth and the pleasure they can bring. All of it erotic but none of it salacious. I had never read such tender fiction, such fiction that treats both the Eucharist and the orgasm with veneration on the page and in the narrative itself.

And that is why, I hope, people will still read Dubus. He knows the body so well. Both man and woman, both able bodied and not. He knows pain and he knows pleasure with a meticulous edge. While I feel that most people reading this essay will have already heard of him—Dubus was often cited as a "writerly writer" and was famous for his workshops in the late 1980s and early 1990s—I do not know if we can see past an easy and reductionist reading of toxic masculinity inherent in both of the institutions he adores (church and military) in a post-pandemic, #MeToo world. Or, if we can see past some of the possible racist, sexist, and/or apologist readings, we can also see in his work. His masculinity is complicated and problematic in some of his stories—but rather than rushing away from those contradictions, I think it's important to sit with them. Not to try and understand them necessarily. But instead, we must become familiar, intimate with these contradictions. To learn from anything—be it a real intruder like racism/sexism or the fictitious one in Dubus' story—we must read the story all the way to the end.

I also hope people still read Dubus because he gave me what I couldn't give myself in those long, early, dark days of postpartum depression: hope in the body. Hope that the body can change, decay, and lose something it once had but still feel both pleasure and pain. In fact, you need both. You need to love that body as much as you hone your mind. Then in that process, maybe whatever you want to call your soul—for me, it is my sons, my husband, the life that was waiting for me on the other side when the dust settled—can emerge.

Eve Morton lives in Waterloo, Ontario, Canada with her partner and two sons. She spends the days running after those boys and the nights brainstorming her next creative project. At some point, she writes things down, usually while drinking copious amounts of coffee. Her most recent novel is *The Serenity Nearby* released in 2022 with Sapphire Books. Find updates at authormorton.wordpress.com.

(pink brain)

by H. Azhar

the autonomic nervous system initiates your 'fight or flight' response. external stimuli (amber eyes, a lopsided smile) trigger the release of hormones (epinephrine, norepinephrine) that mobilize my body to prepare for incoming danger (you).

it has been three years, but my adrenal glands are no more used to you than they were when i was seventeen. i am stuck in a teenager's body, waiting for my heart rate to slow down, waiting for my breath to return. it has been three years, but you show up with child's amusement, amber-turned-gold look-what-the-cat-dragged-in eyes, car playlist in hand, ready to disregard seven months of silence.

i was never good at keeping grudges.

another thing i'm not good at: sleeping. the city has kept me up since i was twelve, wide-eyed and innocent. eight years later, you still fight a nightly battle. each time i pray you'll succeed. my mouth disagrees, it says: *your brain filters your cerebral spinal fluid during sleep. you don't want alzheimer's, do you?* (you can't. i need you around forever). and so every night i stay up, plaque build-up, writing poetry. i drown in cloudy csf. you and your sinuses don't join me.

i try to compartmentalize the brain into something that makes more sense. no more pink, flushed cheeks, headrushes, no— that is simply adrenaline and not love. this euphoria is simply dopamine and not a taste of eden. i am probably not in love with you at all, actually. the hypothalamus is a fickle thing.

the autonomic system initiates your 'fight or flight' response. external stimuli (your hands, on mine) trigger the release of neurotransmitters (dopamine, serotonin) that leave me in a cloud of euphoria (the kind that makes me write nonsense like this). if love is a dance of hormones and synapses, i fell a long time ago.

H. Azhar is a Pakistani-Canadian science student fascinated by the human body and how it manages to feel everything to the extent that it does. When she's not writing, you can find her singing, daydreaming, or impatiently waiting for it to rain.

barren landscape

by Jennifer Mariani

it is not my way
to score my skin
to stain it fickle
as i am
but when you ask what words
i would winnow
or if i would etch or blotch a symbol
somewhere
i remember
others already made
their mark on me
there was a man one summer
with Hebrew slanted
across a perfect shoulder blade
it read
"King of Kings and Lord of Lords"
and when he seared his lips onto mine
i traced that line in memory
but the word of God was on my tongue
always a hymn half sung
what right did my heretic heart have to inscribe
Him on my palms
as He wrote me on His?

in another life i knew so well
i sketched "dancer"
in flowing lines
in whirls
the twirls of an elongated *R* an arm that was a wing
the *N* an arabesque arcing
over the *C*
you see i was someone else then
but i wouldn't be her
now
so i put that word away
until

my daughters were the birthing
of my transcendent self
and if their names were graven on my heart
why not see them blazoned across
my brimming breasts?
yet we are bound
beyond our names
and so i threw them to the speckled stars
i cannot keep
clasping them to me
even as i cling to the love
they bore me

once
i might have scribed the southern stars
upon my lips
in case they coaxed me home
the name of my homeland embroidered into my neck
and if you looked in the cleft behind my knees
you would find all the trees
i yearned to see again

instead
i am left bare
so let me lay myself out
so you can see i am tattooed

here and there
a surgeon's scalpel carved me open
foot and belly, lungs and groin
then left a tapestry with broken bones, babies
and a hole jammed shut
so i could breathe again

there are scars i scrawled along my arms
seeping pain
sorrow running rivers of red
on virgin flesh
shrunken onto bones
brittle from starvation
left to the mercy of a man
who stamped me
with slate-dappled bruises
i am another's page
scribbled across
some unsolved childhood rage
a chapter no longer spoken of

i am left now
in ruins of varicose veins
marks that stretch
that blot the years
of agony
of grief that branded me
in haggard lines

still
in time i think could
rewrite myself
imprint every passage
of every book
that brought me to my knees
and spatter that ink
across my barren landscape
stolen phrases scratched along my ribs
fables engraved into thickened thighs
and stories smudged
along paper-thin fingertips
until i was a living library
till there was nothing left to see
of me

better and better yet
one day every word i have written for you
will streak across my aged skin
those are the emblems i would choose
to keep
to speak
to sing to you
so when you bury me
i will be a love poem
waiting for you
on the other
side

Jennifer Mariani was born and raised in Harare, Zimbabwe. Her first collection of poems *All Forgotten Now*, a chapbook, was published by Off Topic Publishing. Her poetry has also been featured in *Mosi oa Tunya Literary Review*, Uproar (The Lawrence House Centre For The Arts), Off Topic Publishing, The League of Canadian Poets Poetry Pause and Wingless Dreamer anthologies. She has been a guest judge for Off Topic Publishing's monthly poetry contest. Jennifer writes about Africa; both the landscape and being white in post-independent Zimbabwe. She also writes about women's issues including domestic violence, body image and eating disorders. Jennifer currently resides in Calgary, Alberta, with her one partner, two daughters, three cats and numerous volumes of Pablo Neruda's poetry. She teaches ballet and her favourite poems are written for her children.

Soar Spot

by Allison Fradkin

CHARACTERS

DORIS
open age
female-identifying
open ethnicity

WILLONA
open age
female-identifying
open ethnicity

SETTING
The children's playroom of a Safe House for survivors of
domestic violence.

TIME
Late at night, the present.

At rise, DORIS sits at a small table, beading a bracelet.

DORIS
(singing to the tune of "Beat It" by Michael Jackson)
Bead it, bead it / Get yourself a strand and bead it.
(speaking)
Uh-oh. I need a black "I."

(WILLONA pops up from behind a sofa, startling Doris.)

WILLONA
I'm afraid I pull no punches. But I have pulled pranks and
all-nighters. And before you bead me the riot act, I didn't
mean to scare you. Next time, I'll make my presence known in
a fright-free fashion.

DORIS
You will?

WILLONA
Why, yes, I am Will. Short for Willona.

DORIS
I'm Doris. Short—uh, long—for Dor.

WILLONA
As in that thing we claim to walk into whenever we get a
black eye?

DORIS
(holding up a bead)
Well, now that I've got *this* black "I," that excuse is old hat.

WILLONA

Those bracelets for the fundraiser?

DORIS

Yeah. They're all going to say "Survivor." What do you think of
the colour sequence?

WILLONA

Oooh, it's an established pattern, like domestic violence. Clever.

DORIS

What?

WILLONA

It's black and blue, Dor.

DORIS

It's blue and black, Will. Okay, fine, it's… Actually, maybe
that's not such a bad idea. If I make them what you said,
maybe they could act as a distress signal?

WILLONA

Just swap out the blue for the colour purple, okay?
(Doris begins unstringing the bracelet.)
It wasn't a bad idea, though, your blingy SOS.

DORIS

Thanks.

WILLONA

So…I'm guessing this Safe House doubles as a safe space, so
if I shared something like: I was a housewife who became
a can't-leave-the-house wife, you'd tell me something about
yourself, too, right?

DORIS
Sure.

WILLONA
Okay, um…what's your favourite DV movie?

DORIS
That's what you want to know about me? The identity of my
favourite TV movie?

WILLONA
No, I want to know the identity of your favourite DV
movie. Although my favourite DV movie is a TV movie:
A Cry for Help.

DORIS
You enjoy watching movies that hit close to home?

WILLONA
Only when they pack a punch, and this is the punch-packer's
leader. You seen it? It's from 1989. Some chick named Nancy
McKeon plays the victim.

DORIS
Oh, I do know that movie! It came out after *The Facts*.

WILLONA
I think the expression is "after the fact."

DORIS
No, *The Facts of Life*. The TV show? I used to have the biggest
cru…uh, the utmost admiration for her. I'd take the first four
letters of her last name and go:
(*chants and claps to the tune of "Mickey" by Toni Basil*)

Oh, McKe, you're so fine / You're so fine, you blow my mind /
Hey, McKe.
(claps four times)

WILLONA and DORIS
(clap four times)
Hey, McKe.

WILLONA
Why didn't you just replace "Mickey" with "Nancy"? It has the
same number of syllables.

DORIS
Just…wanted to preserve the integrity of the lyrics.

WILLONA
Are you, um… Was your…intimately violent partner…
ladylike?

DORIS
If you consider someone who declines to differentiate between
a fist bump and a knuckle sandwich a lady, then yeah. Anyway,
um, I played Nancy once—the Nancy in the musical *Oliver!*.
She was with a man who…needed her to be his punching bag.

WILLONA
That one I haven't seen. Does she get a "Survivor" bracelet at
the end?

DORIS
Uh, no. No, hers would say…"Victim." That wasn't my
favorite role, but I guess it was good preparation for, um…
my favourite role: Audrey in *Little Shop of Horrors*. She gets a
"Survivor" bracelet.

WILLONA

Okay, that one I have seen, and doesn't she croak at the end?

DORIS

Well, yeah, but not at the hands of her SO.

WILLONA

I think the acronym you're after is "SOB."

DORIS

AKA sob, but there's no use crying over killed milquetoast.
Uh, the SOB ends up expiring and the milquetoast is actually
Seymour, the good guy, and why do I have so much DV on
my CV? I thought the only thing in theatre that's supposed to
get struck is the set.

WILLONA

Looks like I'm going to have to start calling you Stage Dor. Is
that what you did for a living?

DORIS

No, I was just doing it for kicks.

WILLONA

Oh, so you were in *A Chorus Line*.

DORIS

Sort of. Whenever my partner said, "You're gonna get it," I
sang, "I Hope I *Don't* Get It" in my head.

WILLONA

Sing something for me. Out of your head.

DORIS

I'd have to be out of my head to do that because I am
out of practice.

WILLONA

You're safe and sound here, remember? Except without the
sound, you're just "safe and," which sounds like an improv
game hosted by one of your bracelet wearers.

DORIS

Just be glad I'm not making slap bracelets,
(sings to the tune of "My Sharona" by The Knack)
m-m-m-my Willona!

WILLONA

(sings to the tune of the song by Lesley Gore)
You don't own me!

*(They share a laugh, a sound that both delights and
surprises them.)*

WILLONA

You know what I think? I think that each time you leave,
you make a big production of it, don't you? Bet you belt out
"I Am Changing" from *Dreamgirls* before triumphantly
exiting stage left.

DORIS

Close. I went with "Get out and stay out! I'm taking back my
life!" from *9 to 5* before triumphantly exiting stage right.
(Willona stops laughing.)
I was just kidding. I may have considered it, but then I realized
it'd be wiser for me to make a more...unsung departure.

I do sing "I Am Changing" now, though. It's the ultimate
tribute to transformation.

WILLONA

Awww, look at you, thinking you're going to beat the
odds by getting out *and* staying out your first time out.
That's adorable.

DORIS

Batterer up, three strikes, *I'm* out. That's my motto.

WILLONA

Well, bully for you.

DORIS

No bully for me, Will. That's another motto of mine.

WILLONA

You know this is one of those "If at first you don't succeed,
try, try again" type deals, right? Trust me—I'm an old hand
at this. They call it escapism because that's exactly what it is:
a fantasy. And if you somehow managed to turn your fantasy
into a reality, it's only because you had an unfair advantage. I
mean, for you, leaving was child's play, because you and your
partner had...identical identities. No matter how great the
imbalance of power was between the two of you, you were
still equals. Plus, you never had to worry about being
unexpectedly expectant.

DORIS

Are you—

WILLONA

So you can quit singing your praises, Dor. In fact, *I am changing* the station, because I'd really like to listen to something a little less infuriatingly inspirational, okay?

DORIS

Sorry.

WILLONA

So now you want to play games with me?

DORIS

What?

(Willona plucks the board game "Sorry!" off a shelf and plops it onto the table.)

DORIS

Oh, "Sorry!" Not…sorry.

WILLONA

Ah, sorry-not-sorry, excuse extraordinaire for the unapologetically unapologetic.

DORIS

Yeah. I wonder who invented that phrase.

WILLONA

Probably a wife beater in a wife beater. Too bad that's not really their traditional costume. If *my* guy had been wearing that when I first met him, I could've beaten a hasty retreat.

DORIS

Will, what's the opposite of a playlist?

WILLONA

A...don't-playlist?

DORIS

A don't-playlist, perfect. That's exactly what this fundraiser
needs, and I am putting that song there.

WILLONA

Which song?

DORIS

The one you just mentioned: "My Guy." It's hardly uplifting.
(sings to the tune of "My Guy" by Mary Wells)
I'm tellin' you from the start / I can't be torn apart from
my guy.

WILLONA

It can be uplifting—with some updating.
(sings, same tune)
I'm tellin' you from the start / I can't be torn apart *by* my guy.

DORIS

Now *that* is the proper preposition. I don't even care that
the lyrics don't apply to...Sapphic arrangements. I care, but
I like the song "My Girl" better anyway because there's no
temptation more irresistible than appreciation.

WILLONA

Oooh, we should have a survivors' sing-along! We come up
with new lyrics for the songs on the don't-play list and then we
drop the "don't."

84

DORIS

What a sound *system* that would be: inspirational speakers
accompanying our inspirational speakers!

WILLONA

You really like my idea, Dor? You're not yanking my chain?

DORIS

We'll be yanking our own chains off completely one day, but
today we're yanking "Chains" by The Cookies off the don't-
play list and making it into…

WILLONA

"Change" by The Tough Cookies!
(sings to the tune of "Chains" by The Cookies)
Can run around / 'Cause I'm now free.
(speaking)
I like that. It might be tricky with some songs, though—like
that BS song, although we could try something like:
(sings to the tune of "One More Time" by Britney Spears)
"Hit me, baby, no more times." Oh! How about
(sings to the tune of "Hit Me With Your Best Shot" by Pat Benatar)
"Hit me with your best shot / I'll hit the road!"
(speaking)
Or are those last two too similar?

DORIS

Not at all. Repetition is key. A person hears something often
enough, she starts to believe it, and when she takes the good,
then shakes the bad…

WILLONA

(sings to the tune of "He's Got the Power" by The Exciters)
He's got no power / No power no more / Over me.

DORIS
Who's the infuriatingly inspirational one now, Will? Hey,
what's the name of the group that sings that again?

WILLONA
The Exciters.

DORIS
What do you say we drop the C and be The Exiters?

WILLONA
I'd get a kick out of it.

DORIS
You watch your phraseology!

WILLONA
Excuse me?

DORIS
That's from *The Music Man*.

WILLONA
I'd rather hear what The Music Woman has to say.

DORIS
Well, she says—

WILLONA
She?
(*teasingly tossing an "I" bead at Doris*)
Don't be crying your "I's" out.

DORIS
Fine.
(teasingly tossing the bead back at Willona)
I'll just narrow my beady little "I's" at you instead. Okay, so
we're definitely putting "*I* Am Changing" on the play list, as-is,
plus "Raise Your Voice" from *Sister Act*, and what do you think
about adding Sofia's song from *The Color Purple*?

WILLONA
Oh, "Hell No"!

DORIS
Really? I would've thought that you… Wait, did you mean hell
yes to "Hell No"?

WILLONA
Hell yes to hell yes to "Hell No." That song would really hit
the spot right now. Well, not the *sore* spot. But a song about
refusing to be cruising for a bruising can really encourage
a person to make tracks, you know? Some days I had it on
repeat, while I fantasized about asserting myself. I even started
singing it out loud. One time he overhead me. I crooned, he
cringed—and criticized.

WILLONA (continued)
(imitating her abuser)
"I know why the caged bird sings. She's a Maya Ange-loser.
Awww, don't pout, Willona. You know I'm only teasing, and
still, I get a rise out of you."
(as if addressing him)
And what do I ever get out of you, huh? Nothing but
another bouquet of your sorry-not-sorry-ass flowers, perfect
for playing that time-honoured game of "He Shoves Me, He
Shoves Me Not."

(coming back to reality)

Oh my goodness. Dor, I am so…I apologize for going off on you like that. I think I'll…I guess I'll go back to…yeah.

(Willona starts for the door.)

DORIS

You don't have to go back, Will.

WILLONA

To my room or to my doom?

(Doris rushes to the door and blocks it.)

DORIS

Look, if you even think about going back to him, I will slap you silly.

WILLONA

Oh, will you now? Because you know what they say: "Don't let the Dor hit you."

DORIS

Sorry. Sorry. Not-free. I mean, sorry, sincerely, without the "not."

WILLONA

Look, I just want to go back—

DORIS
Will—

88

WILLONA

—to my room, and listen to music or something until I
fall asleep.

DORIS

What are you going to listen to, hmm? Something off
her Greatest Hits album? Like the gritty little ditty
"Diss You Much"?

WILLONA

No, I'm going to pop in *his* Greatest Hits album, which
includes the scintillating single "You Can't Stop the
Beatdown." Except we can. And we did. Because where there's
a *Will*, there's a way out of the non-revolving *Dor*. And guess
what? I've been making my own Greatest Hits album—photo,
not record. This way, I'll have a record of...everything.
(crosses behind the sofa and retrieves a photo album)
What, you think you're the only crafty one around here? Well,
you're not. Check out the sparkly letter stickers on the cover.

DORIS
(reading the cover)
"Domestic Abuse Goddess." Ah, so now *you* want to play
games with *me*. Pac-Man in particular. Short for Pack-Your-
Bags-and-Leave-That-Man. You already won, Will. You don't
need a rematch, just a better match—someday if that's
what you want.
(Doris holds her hand out, palm down. Willona stares at it.)
Don't high-fives make suitably silly slaps? Okay, so it's a low-five.

WILLONA

Because you'd never raise a hand to your Willona.
(low-fives her)
Ugh, we are going to be insufferable, aren't we?

DORIS
I think the adjective you're after is "inseparable."

(Doris opens her arms for a hug. Willona accepts—but not without making a big production of how accommodating and sacrificial she's being.)

WILLONA
This must be how Woodstock feels when Snoopy hugs him, except I don't feel all that small.

DORIS
Consider me your emotional support frenemy.

WILLONA
If you start singing "anyone you can leave, I can leave faster," I will leave. For good. I mean it.

DORIS
Looks like I'm going to have to start calling you Mali-boo-boo Barbie, batterer no longer included. When you peel off her bandages, her boo-boos disappear, thanks to water-activated colour-changing technology.

WILLONA
You mean water-*de*activated. Because underneath the coat of war paint we apply to the bruises is a brave face just waiting to be put on.

DORIS
Eventually those bruises will be gone-but-not-forgotten, and we'll think of them as souvenirs of survival. They'll still be a sore spot, but we'll be able to spell that word a little differently.

WILLONA
S-O-A-R?

DORIS
Hell yes.
(They begin beading bracelets together.)
Hey, Will, are you really, um…?

WILLONA
Beading for two? Yeah. And since I don't want to get a beating
for two, I suppose I'd better see this…uprooting to the end.

DORIS
Well, as you can see, *I'm* up rooting for you.

WILLONA
(sings to the tune of "I Am Changing" from Dreamgirls)
Look at us.

DORIS
(sings, same tune)
We are beading, beading bracelets 'cause we can.

WILLONA
(sings, same tune)
We are beading, better off without that man.
(speaking)
Or that woman.

DORIS
(sings, same tune)
But I need you.

WILLONA
You skipped a little, but I'll let it slide, like a bead onto a
string.
(sings, same tune)
I need you.

DORIS and WILLONA
(sings, same tune)
I need a hand / Not a black eye / To see everything so clear…

Curtain.

Allison Fradkin (she/her/hers) delights in applying her Women's & Gender Studies education to the creation of prose, poems, and plays that enlist their characters in a caricature of the idiocies and intricacies of insidious isms. Her work has been published in *Voyage, Chaotic Merge, Limina: A Journal of Historical and Cultural Studies, Flash 405, Fterota Logia, ImageOutWrite, Pastel Serenity,* and *Sapphic Writers Collective.* An enthusiast of inclusivity and accessibility, Fradkin freelances for her hometown of Chicago as Literary Manager of Violet Surprise Theatre, curating new works by queer playwrights; and as Dramatist for Special Gifts Theatre, adapting scripts for actors of all abilities.

Dispatches from the Womb

by Désirée Jung

Everything said here will be true except for the fiction that permeates all the facts once an eye addresses them. This will be your story. This will be your life's retelling of how, despite all contrary evidence, you will be undesired by your father before you are born. You will learn this much later, though. Your life won't be easy. At times, you will be angry and confused. You will try—unsuccessfully—to escape the destiny imposed on you until eventually coming to terms with its direct relationship to names.

When this testimony arrives at the tip of your fingers, you will be typing your past into the future. You will get here, as you know, with my aid. I will help you write the story of how you will be your mother's second attempt to give birth, successfully this time. You will understand how she will desire what you will become—even though you won't know that just yet.

You will also comprehend how she will know, consciously or not, the weight (and the power) this child will carry if she survives her death, and her father's desire never to have children. Your mother will give you a name that will help you survive his death wish, and this name will help you live, despite him not wanting you to. From this moment on, and this same inscription, you will know the truth around names—when you are ready to listen.

When you enter your father's house for the first time, you won't understand why you won't feel loved by him and feel rejected instead. You will conclude there is something wrong with you.

You will accept his rules and hear him saying several times during your lifespan, as though joking: "you are your mother's daughter. I have nothing to do with you."

As a baby, you will cry only in silence to not upset your father. Can't you see I am burning inside? You will want to say. Can't you see my death in your eyes? You will attempt to hurl. You will feel this rejection coming from all parts without necessarily knowing why.

For a long time, you won't talk about it, or write with your own words, until here and now. But one day, you will survive your father's desire to kill you from life.

You will search for the meaning of fatherhood your entire existence, even as you watch your mother die and reflect on how she loved and desired you.

You will never be welcomed in your father's house, not even to this day.

You will acknowledge he was never physically abusive to any of you, though sometimes you will wish he were. You will hear this described as a terrible thing, especially when you don't know how cruelty, coldness, and psychological oppression can also be considered abuse and attempted control.

You will understand the constellations of your origins. You will recognize your father as an imposed impostor. You will never have children for fear of projecting this horrific rejection to another child. You will spend much of your life in solitude, learning how to cope with your own history. You will be able to arrive here and write this acknowledgement. You will type this page from a much lighter place.

You will sympathize with the daughter portrayed in the movie *Imitation of Life* who confronts her mother about the meaning of ever being born. Like her, you will no longer need your mother's reasons to live—you will have found your own. You will retell your past. You will recognize how your mother tried to compensate for your father's lack of presence. You will feel loved by her. You will learn how your father's father had a fulminant heart attack when he was fourteen. You will also hear from your aunts how your father found his father's body in the kitchen—an alcoholic accountant who gambled all his money and hit his son. Your father will have tears in his eyes when he speaks about his father. His sisters will tell you the true story.

As the eldest child of a low-income family, your father will help his mother, your grandmother, to raise three siblings: his first take on fatherhood, unaccounted.

Based on this, you will try to justify your father's rejection of you. You will repeat your mother's discourse to persuade you of your father's conduct. You will acknowledge the profound after effects this narrative will have on you, and you will not be convinced by it. You will stop repeating this same story to justify his behaviour. You will also speculate on how your father unconsciously might have wished for his own father's death— like you—and the surfaced guilt when it materialized in front of him. You will see how being unwanted hides another veiled side of desire: the carrier of death and rejection. You will grasp how this logic also predetermined your birth.

Your sexuality will be a huge source of conflict. For the longest time, you will try to avoid facing the love and hatred you feel around women and their relationships with men without necessarily knowing why. Your sexual desire for women, and your affectionate love for a man who never wanted you in the first place, will literally cut your mind to pieces.

You will not know about orgasm until much later, yet not fully. You will tend to associate sex with death and psychosis.

You will have a difficult time differentiating satisfaction from unsatisfaction, pleasure from displeasure, enjoyment from abuse. You will have several passages through psychiatric wards. You will be held under the Canadian Mental Health Act. You will act desperate, lost, until you get here.

You will have a long road ahead of you when you decide to talk to someone who will listen. Your work with her will last for several years (still unfinished), and this labour will bring you back to words. You will anchor your fears in your writing and learn how to express yourself. You will talk about your sense of rupture. You will re-experience your feeling of rejection. You will reconnect with the profound feeling of desire you received from your mother. You will be more tolerant and understanding towards other people's sufferings. You will see how many people, not just you, feel likewise. You will relate this uneasiness with fatherhood.

You will find examples in literature. In Karl Ove Knausgaard's autobiographical fiction, he describes drinking sour milk with cereal for fear of displeasing his father as a boy, swallowing that terrible taste in silence. You will identify with his eagerness to be loved by this father. You will retell the metaphor of the sour milk and its unsettling taste as the perfect match for your feelings around your father. You will realize your father's horror before your efforts, unaware of why you underwent such extensive pains. You will learn how to say no and not pay any price in exchange for love. You will know this truth after recollecting several painful events you experienced intimately.

You will recall when you tried to say no to a boyfriend who forced himself on you, raping you the first time you ever had sex with a man. You will find it difficult to rewrite these events as they truly happened. You will also remember other men you had sex with, without truly wanting to, partially because you didn't know how to say no. You will also recollect a relationship with a woman who was physically and emotionally abusive to you. You will question yourself on why you held the role of the victim.

You will associate victimhood with fatherhood. You won't take these answers for granted and will suffer a lot to understand the meaning of all this. You will realize that only by naming your past will you be able to change your relationship to the future, despite the hurt it may inflict on you at times. You will be comforted by the memory of your mother's stunning beauty and kind eyes. You will also recognize her Medusa-like presence, paralyzing and unspeakable, turning men into ashes before anyone could name them. You will reflect on her power to stop words midair, at her own liking, even if that silence could cost her life in the end. You will become aware of your mother's unconscious revenge against patriarchy, imposed and inherited on her as well.

You will also have the chance to meet her serpents, whom you will take a liking to and appreciate quite well: crawling from head-to-head, unwanted, and yet traversing generations without stop, before entering yours, while your father will remain a lifelong believer of universal truths, a true mathematician. One day, reflecting on the possibility of being his most irrational number, you will hear a laugh surfacing in the deepest parts of you. This laugh will be a mysterious and unheard voice. You will welcome it for the first time, meeting the unaccounted dead baby girl living inside your guts.

Before she can speak her name, you will apologize for never acknowledging her existence before. You will tell her you are ready to listen, knowing how her unbearable truths will affect you. You will hear her laugh again, this time with true excitement. And you will smile back at her with an open heart.

You will become the first woman in your family to invite a dead baby to your bed to listen to what she will have to say. You will open her eyes as she lies lifeless inside you, slowly awakening to life just because you desired to listen to her stories, in and out of your dreams. You will get to know her deepest wishes, her greatest strengths, and will learn how they are all tied together to your collective fears. You will also be delighted to finally have the chance to greet her, while she will be enchanted to finally have the courage to voice herself out to you. You, too, will tell her about your secrets, and the fright you've always felt about being a woman. With her help, you will learn how to trust your feelings and let go of her protective, but deadly, placenta.

You will name the effects of your childhood and their self-produced punishments. You will see how numbing your emotions is like inserting needles under your skin, a mass, a colourless acid, lactic formed like sour milk and produced in the muscle tissues during strenuous exercise. You will tell her: "no wonder I have been feeling exhausted lately," to which she will reply, "no wonder the memory has a bad taste, it's the return of nausea from your birth." You will love her to death until she becomes part of you. You will grieve her loss in your letters. At last, you will remind yourself always to breathe deeply, but especially at night, not conceding to your father's deadly wish.

You will not let his death devastate you, nor let your desire die. You will know about your death from inside out, which will be your source of light. You will be pleased by life's small pleasures, like the golden sunshine glow of the first days of spring. You will carry your history with pride. Despite the sorrows it contains within. You will know the meaning of your name by heart, comprehending how to move beyond your mother's graph. You will be here until you are not, for this is not up for you to chart.

Désirée Jung is an artist and illustrator from Vancouver, Canada. Most of her literary work and art have been published worldwide, as well as her series of video poems, screened in several film festivals, and available on you tube. Her most recent book *Meu Jeito de Viver*, has been published by Editora Selo in Brazil, 2022. For more information, check her website: desireejung.com.

New Novenas

by Bethanie Humphreys

I.

Your ankles' gentle swells—
gladiolus bulbs

II.

For the scars beneath your stubborn chin—
I give thanks

III.

Poiesis inks your wrist's tender underside—
come, create with me

IV.

Fairy hollows behind your knees—
kettle tea steeping

V.

Your kiss—
August car's black leather seats

VI.

Dipping fingers in a sack of slick beans—
susurrus

VII.

Kitten nestles his bullet-head in your hand's cup—
smaller gods ask no less

VIII.

Your head on my shoulder, my legs bridge your hips,
your thighs tucked against me—fox pose

IX.

Listening when you say—
what happened to you wasn't your fault

Cerith Shell

by Bethanie Humphreys

You
surely
formed
in a cerith's
confines;
slender,
elongated,
with pointed
spire, pink-
tongued your
way through
the many
whorls,
welled
into
curve
of bone
until
you
stretched
into
air

I lie
around
you, my fingers
tracing poems
down your
arms, your
spine,
pour
into your
hips'
whorls,
pink
tongue
my way
into
curve,
bone,
until you
stretch
into
air

Ode to the Clavicle

by Bethanie Humphreys

Sweet, sibilant
s-shaped horizon

fairy hollow bookends

if I were a bird
you would be
my wishbone

you allow my arms
to dangle freely
when I can resist
crossing them

not all bones
can be touched
like you

not all bones
want you to

we have two
but not
for sharing

you serve as struts
shoulder blades
to sternum

first
to break
when you take
the fall

clavicula - Latin
for little key
that turns on your axis
when I lift my arms
to fly

Bethanie Humphreys is a late-blooming lesbian from Sacramento, California. She is a writer, editor, mixed-media visual artist, and educator. Former Editor-in-Chief of the *American River Review* and Associate Editor and Art Director for *Tule Review*, her work has appeared in the U.S. and U.K., including: *Poetry Foundation, Artemis, Nonbinary Review*, and *Found Poetry Review*. Her chapbook, *Dendrochronology*, was published by Finishing Line Press in 2019. She is a California Certified Naturalist, and Amherst Writers and Artists method instructor. She leads various workshops including: poetry editing, science-inspired poetry, and a guided National Poetry Writing Month experience. Learn more at: bethaniehumphreys.com

Interview With My Body

by Emma Května

Tell me why
only you

can do this job.

Because I don't
remember a time

when I've
felt comfortable

in you. It started
as a child.

The capacity
to *be,*

Quite simply—

before you

there was me. But

there's never been
a moment

long enough
to express the power

I truly possess.

Fearful of never
getting the chance,

and yet do so
little about it.

I never forget anything
you experience;

When things don't
work out, please
know

only minds do that. Your
chariot in the world,

I must
—if needed—

my wisdom guides you
where you need be.

trust where
I want to go.

Emma Května is a Canadian writer and poet with UK and Czech roots, currently living in Nova Scotia on the traditional territory of the Mi'kmaq Nation. Her work has appeared in *Filling Station, Planisphere Quarterly*, Bell Press, and *FAYD Digital.* In 2019, her fiction was shortlisted in a UK writing contest. Emma is also a creative writing teacher, musician, artist, and host of the podcast *Wild Creative.*

Joanne, I'll Pray for You

by Rachel Lachmansingh

You and Julian are dating, but yesterday you buzzed into his apartment complex, took the elevator six floors up, turned right and then left and then right again, knocked on apartment 650, and broke up with him. Quickly. I'm possessed, is all you said when he asked why. He still wore his comic-printed boxers, his hair unbrushed, teeth milky.

Julian is a nice guy. Julian is a nice guy because he cooks tandoori tacos and sushi donuts. Julian is a nice guy because he's training in acupuncture and practices on you whenever you want. Julian is a nice guy because he takes you to the drive-in, kisses you to old Swedish movies and gifts you ripped mixtapes all named after things you were interested in three years ago when you first started dating (*Tunisian Crochet*, *Expired Film*, *Dining Etiquette*).

Blocks from his apartment, you wait until the traffic clears to jaywalk to the cathedral you visit every Sunday. Cars whir; stoplights refract off the stained-glass windows. Winter slush fills your runners and you want to cuss but it's a busy street. You alternate between nibbling the six-dollar pastry you bought and smoking the last of a cigarette.

Two women from the Salvation Army are stationed in front of the cathedral's steps. Santa rings a bell, off-tempo, behind them. You should donate. Julian would donate. You don't make eye contact as you flick your cigarette butt at the sidewalk and hike up the staircase.

Inside, you take off your shoes and empty the slush next to the front door's white donation box. Someone important—a priest, a deacon, whoever works at a church—pauses in front of you, frowns and then moves on. You hope that man slips on it the next time he circles around. When you realize this is probably anti-Christian, you dip your fingers in the holy water at the archway and cross yourself just as you've watched other patrons do.

You're not religious but come here often, ever since a poltergeist found you nearly two years ago at a college party and never left. Now, the choir members recognize you and wave when you stay for mass—Hi Joanne, I've been praying for you. When they sing the hymns, hallelujah, hallelujah, you tune out and trace the outlines of the altar's candles with your pointer finger. You recite prayers a beat behind everyone else because you still haven't memorized them, your voice delayed like a demonic chant. The family behind you always moves. It's a different one every time, but they always do.

*

Magdalena sat with you for five minutes today. She is almost eighty and reminds you of your grandmother. Sometimes she brings you dhal puri and mithai to make sure you're eating. She tells you to stop smoking and has her son buy you nicotine patches, powdered ginseng and thumbs of fresh ginger (she really thinks you'll just eat it?). Since the poltergeist first appeared nearly two years ago, Magdalena has sat with you every Sunday. She gifts you these offerings in neat paper bags, everything wrapped in waxed paper and your name written in careful up-percase on the front—*JOANNE.*

You have never told Julian about her. Today, you talked to her about the breakup. Magdalena listens, her ankles crossed under the pew. You don't know exactly why you ended it, but theorize it was the poltergeist. It must have slid into your body at four and stayed there until you got up two hours later, hair in a frizz, pyjamas still on, and drove to Julian's apartment com-plex—no socks. Magdalena hushes you when you get angry—that fucking ghost—but doesn't stop you from finishing. Today, you somehow hate Julian; maybe you have for a while. Just like you hate this city, which once shimmered silver and now only seems grey. Magdalena has never denied that you're haunted even though her eyes, blueish with age, say something else. Her voice is gentle when she speaks, and echoes off the domed ceil-ing. Talk to someone, she says. My son can get you a number.

*

At home, you blow your nose in the Kleenex you'd bought from Costco. At the time, you felt grown up because you bought your Kleenex in bulk from Costco—what other twenty-year-old does that? You keep them in your closet, piled carefully, like Jenga, and pull out the boxes you think are prettiest whenever one runs out.

You should get a new apartment. Your unit is basically furniture-less, with a double mattress kicked in the corner and a dining table with one chair offsetting the kitchen. Julian tried decorating the walls with his photographs from New Zealand, Zimbabwe, and some coastal towns in Italy. But you didn't have tape and you hated the pictures, how colourful they were (you didn't tell him this; instead, said, Julian, we don't have tape; he frowned). A stack of them lie kicked in the corner where a couch should be. Outside, it has begun to flurry, and you hate the city in the winter, you hate the city's rumble in your apartment. You hate the city, period.

Julian has tried to call you. You see the notification as you reach for your phone. You're inclined to google how to sublet an apartment, how much it'll cost to break your lease and what to do when you can't unfeel a stranger's palms on your arms, collarbones, thighs. But also can't help but feel those same hands move you when you brush your teeth when nauseous, when you sit, barefoot, in your dark bathroom, holding your arms around shoulders that no longer feel like yours.

You feel body-less and desperately want a cigarette, or a drink. But there's nothing in the fridge. There's nothing in the cabinets. You google if it's possible to use the expired packets of yeast in your baking cabinet to make beer overnight. You google if the alcohol in mouthwash will give you the same relief as the alcohol in 80-proof vodka. You google Julian's address and run your finger along the blue line between your place and his. You google why when you first moved here, you woke naked on a rainy morning in a bed that wasn't yours, lost in the jumble of drinks, and stumbled home trembling and barefoot. You google why since then, a poltergeist has clung to your back, made your body its own. You google why you hate Magdalena's mithai even though they're the best thing you've eaten since moving here. You google why you cry when staring at the ceiling of your bedroom too long, why it feels like a black hole, gaping, waiting for you to reach out and touch it. You call Julian back.

*

He brings you a cup of coffee and a cinnamon bun. They were your favourite when you started dating back in high school, before Julian moved to this city for college, before you cared enough to follow him right after you graduated. You don't touch the coffee but break off a piece of the cinnamon bun to please him. When he's not looking, you stick it into the pocket of your jeans because you don't want to eat it. You can't. Your mouth doesn't work. It's useless on your face and you want to cut it off with an Exacto knife.

Despite your breakup, Julian shows up every morning at eleven with coffee and a cinnamon bun. He sets them both on your barren kitchen counter and claps when you pick them up. You never eat them and stick them in your closet with the tissue boxes. After two weeks, there's an entire pile of them in there, sticky and mouldy and smelling so good but also horrifying. You never question why he still cares for you, what he gets out of it, if this is just what it's like to be a good person. He drives you to the cathedral every week and sits there in the parking lot while you talk to Magdalena in five-minute bursts like you always do. She says, My son tells me deep breathing might help you. Julian brings you more cinnamon buns. You start throwing the cups of coffee into the houseplant he buys for your place (he read plants exhale dopamine on *Yahoo! Answers* which is a lie, but he's desperate to make you feel better).

None of it works, of course, and Julian starts noticing the foul stink of cinnamon coming from your closet when you lie in bed together, untouching. One night, when he believes you're asleep, he turns into his pillow and gasps. It takes you too long to realize he is crying, which only makes you feel worse. Your visits to the cathedral wane. Magdalena's son tries to reach out, but you never answer his phone calls, though, on one of your last visits to the cathedral, you leave a note by her pew before she arrives, a barren *Thank you*. When you come home from a walk and Julian's in the kitchen whipping butter and cinnamon sugar into a pulpy, gluey mess—more cinnamon buns—you collapse at the table and cry.

The smell is making you nauseous, you explain when he tries to soothe you. And when he goes to throw the whole thing out, you add, It's not bad, it's not bad. And you sob miserably.

*

Julian lets you be alone. He heads back to his apartment and promises he'll spend the night googling more remedies that probably won't help you, but will try, nonetheless. Some part of you knows he cries the moment he steps out of your place. Some part of you wonders what would happen if you told him to stop coming around.

At your kitchen table, you peck at a microwave dinner. The city's skyline blurs as the snow falls. In your pocket is the number Magdalena's son really did find for you. Some generic hotline, *1-800-722-4378*. You wouldn't have to tell them who you are. You could lie. You could say your name is Jada, not Joanne, and they would never know. You could say you have blue eyes, not brown, and they would believe you. You could be a different person. Tell the operator you've found wholeness, that your body revels in it. Never tell them about Julian's cinnamon buns, moulding in your closet, or the poltergeist and how it broke you, about Magdalena's generosity that feels undeserved. You could just pretend. And yet, you don't take out the paper but remember the number anyway, punch it into your cellphone after you've made it through an eighth of the soggy meatloaf and bring your knees to your chest because you're scared. When the line rings, then transfers to hold music, then to the soft voice of a woman saying, *Thank you for calling, my name is Sandra, how can I assist you today?* you hang up and press a hand to your chest.

Rachel Lachmansingh is a Guyanese-Canadian writer from Toronto. Her writing has appeared in *Minola Review*, *Grain Magazine*, *The Malahat Review*, *The New Quarterly*, *The Fiddlehead*, and *The Puritan*, among others. She was longlisted for the 2022 CBC Short Story Prize and is currently pursuing her BA in creative writing.

St. Marks Orgy Room, 1981

by Alejo Rovira Goldner

chest, mouth, muscle, tongue, hand, nipple, skin,
neck, sole, cheek, arm, nail, skin, tatt, pits,
voice, smell, voice, liquor, heel, penis, heel, nodule,
face, skin, adam's apple, hair, back, front, fist,
hair, leg, ring finger, skin, earlobe, tongue, liver spots,
anus, leg, skin, liquor, penis, liquor, semen-cake,
cut, uncut, anus, quaalude, face, muscle, testes,
lip, ankle, tongue, eyelid, elbow, penis, face-fag,
head, moustache, navel, skin, kidney, liver,
white cells, lung, liver, pavlov, skin, heart, nerve,
id, ego, liver, lung, lip-skin, cockroach, eye-kiss
skin, brown skin, black skin, tongue, facial, fecal,
liver, amygdala, nostril, crab louse, liver, ear-kiss,
groin, gland, night sweat, mouth, beard, forehead, liver,
heart, lip, heart, poppers, heart, penis, river, sperm,
white cells, celebration, shoulder blade, brain wrinkle,
shin, spine, pore, eye, knuckle, spine, liver, eye, id,
shin, celebration, poppers, kiss, kool & the gang,
calves, lick, kick, party, poppers, id, liver-sick, id,
pancreas, darrell, pelvis, steve, ramón, finger

white cells, white skin, brown skin, black skin, lip-skin,
lung, smell, lung-smell, rectum, nose, rectum, tongue,
tooth, lung, rectum-kiss, joy, poppers-joy, party-joy,
sarcoma, cheek, hole, party-hole, penis, ambulance,
skin, sweat, sarcoma, lung, toenail, sweat, sarcoma
finger, cell count, belly, lust, waist, penis-rust,
arteries, hands, brain, liver-sick, brain-sick, tissue-sick,
lip, groin, david, surgeon, rust, eduardo, dust, i.c.u,
cancer, jaw, cancer, jew, nurse, cancer, wasp, muslim,
bladder, rapture, doctor, nurse, church mass, rupture,
barry, marcellus, peter, jaime, john, jerome, myles,
paul, avery, jackson, phideau, enrique, philip, pedro,
hand, thigh, soul-kiss, skull-kiss, mortician, soil-kiss,
needle, heart, the sign of the cross, rabbi, priest, eulogy,
mouth, church mass, doctor, eyebrow, scalpel, last rites,
chest, mouth, muscle, tongue, tooth, nipple-skin, lip,
neck, sole, cheek, arm, bear, chicken hawk, pit, penis,
smell, liquor, liquor-smell, penis, pelvis, pore, sore,
skin, adam's apple, hair, nipple, poppers, tongue,
nostril, nipple, navel, poppers, love.

Alejo Rovira Goldner left Spain in the 1990s to settle in Southern California. He has published in *The Antioch Review*, *The Harvard Gay and Lesbian Review*, *Otoliths* and *The Los Angeles Review of Los Angeles*, among other journals, usually under the name "Alex M. Frankel." His most recent book is a story collection, *Flame at Door and Raisin*, which Kirkus has described as "powerfully haunting tales of love, betrayal, and heartbreak in the Europe of decades past."

Fat Girl's Dinner Party

by Kali Meister

Buffalo Bill calls me a big girl.
      (In retaliation, I eat a pint of Häagen-Dazs—
           that'll show him.)

If you had your way, would you kill me
in a basement with a bucket and a miniature dog?
My round rosy rump and back haunches will make a fine Sunday
suit, side panels and an elastic waistband,
                        roomy.

Serial killers make lousy lovers,
whittling away in my soft pudgy thighs,
        friction more than fucking.
My breathing is shallow and fine,
no skipping heartbeats,
not even a flushed face when he finally cums.

Inside Bill's hole in the basement floor
I am a woman with needs, a Rubenesque beauty.
Tonight I demand Bill take me out in public.
I wear a dress that flatters the plump of my bottom lip,
        strapless
           silk to hug my doughy belly.

My erect nipples pique the interest of Ted Bundy,
Table Two in the corner. Tonight Bill and I get the best seats in
the place.

I eat dessert first.

I am the show, the murderers' feast.
They dine on elbows, waving arm rolls—
the insides of my knees are this evening's special,
          with a side of delicious rack.

I am the appetizer and main course until she arrives,
acid tripping angel on a bad day.
Aileen Wuornos screams, "Sure, you can fuck her,
          but do any of you love her?"

The Boston Strangler puts down his pantyhose as he wipes his
mouth clean.

Kali Meister's writing is an extension of her rich experiences in theatre, performance art, and film. In the many theatrical productions to her credit, Meister has worked as a playwright, director, actor, costume coordinator, and make-up designer. She has performed as a poet, storyteller, and stand-up comic.

Her literary achievements include winning the 2005 Margaret Atley Woodruff Award for fiction and the 2006 Margaret Atley Award for playwriting. She also received the 2005 and 2006 Eleanor Burke Award for non-fiction from the University of Tennessee's English department. Meister's poetry, fiction, non-fiction, and dramatic writing, has been featured in publications such as *Circle Magazine*, *Pegasus Review*, *Outscapes*, *34 Orchard*, and *Phoenix*. Her play *After Autumn* was a featured finalist in the 2010 Appalachian Festival of Plays and Playwrights in Abingdon, VA, at Barter Theater.

She produces, writes, directs, and acts in short films under her production company SheWonder Productions. Her films focus on the female experience, female narrative, and female talent.

from Abridged Notes of a Porn Addict

by Alton Melvar M Dapanas

Van Wylde and his twisted dick are about to ejaculate. After countless buffering, and 30 minutes spent watching a 15-minute clip, I reach the quintessential stroke, finally. As if the world will end without it. And in my three-second brain freeze, the world feels like it is going to end without it. But there is a feeling of unease *after*. I close the browser tabs, horrified as if I wasn't the one who opened them.

During hookups, I always wish the stranger comes first; if I do, I mentally push their bodies away, repulsing every second of it. This disgust, to me, someone who prefers positions allowing more skin contact, still does not make sense.

Dominant in the streets, submissive in the sheets was my Planet Romeo bio back then.

When asked by Pulitzer Prize-winning journalist Chris Hedges what are the signs if a man is a porn addict, former porn actress Shelley Luben said, "They're shut down. They can't look me in the eyes. They can't be intimate." Luben now runs a Christian outreach program for women formerly in porn.

The 2016 guidebook *Getting Started with NoFap* lists: (1) "increase in porn use over time" (from once a week to several times a day) (2) "increase in the intensity of the porn used" (watching genres that used to disgust you, (3) "inability to stop using pornography despite negative consequences" as signs of porn addiction. The simplified version is the Four Cs: Compulsion to watch porn; Continue to use porn despite negative effects on their life; inability to Control the consumption; and Craving it when not watching one.

At least eight books—mostly genre fiction—have characters who have the same addiction: new adult romances Novoneel Chakraborty's *Marry Me, Stranger* and Cherry Lola's *Porn Star*, thrillers Lisa Unger's *In The Blood* and John Sandford's *Silken Prey*, G.A. Hauser's collection of erotic stories *In The Dark*, the *Serial Killers* series by Jack Rosewood, and *The Spellman* series by Lisa Lutz, as well as Lidia Yuknavitch's feminist retelling *Dora: A Headcase*.

I felt seen. Particularly in essays—"Sex and Cancer: A History in Three Parts," an excerpt from Luke Ryan's comedy memoir *A Funny Thing Happened on the Way to Chemo* and anthologized in *The Best Australian Essays 2014* as well as "Travels in Pornland" by Andrea Stuart, first published in *Granta* and anthologized in *The Best American Essays 2017*.

My favourite of all, a memoir, came with the subtitle "one woman's journey through sex and porn addiction." In *Getting Off* (2018), Mexican-American essayist Erica Garza confesses her favourite scene "of all time involves two sweaty women, fifty horny men, a warehouse, a harness, a hair dryer, and a taxicab." She uses the adjectives *revolting, sickening* and *disgusting* but admittedly unable to stop. As for me, my favourite scene is none. But the archetypes of clips I jerk off to come under three tropes: (1) Someone petite and someone huge hovering over the petite like SayUncle.com or BBC (not the British media network) or Tiny4k. *Is this my subconscious need to be protected?* (2) someone old dominating, or getting dominated by someone younger like those with tags MILFs or DILFs or

Japanese mature. *Is this my innate fear of growing old and staying young?* (3) edging videos where someone gets "milked." (See more on #alter Twitter or OnlyFans.) *Dominant in the streets, submissive in the sheets* right there.

For our next session, I will ask one of my writing mentors: *Is there a correlation between porn addiction and Anglophone essayists?* For our next session, I will ask my therapist: *How can I be addicted to something I find revolting, sickening, disgusting after doing it?*

In *Your Brain in Porn: Internet Pornography and the Emerging Science of Addiction,* controversial "anti-porn" writer Gary Wilson posits that the most common roots of porn addiction are boredom, sexual frustration, loneliness and stress. I wonder if the generation of queer men before me, with their video rentals and late-night cable channels, were as bored or more fucked up. Sex therapist and public policy analyst Marty Klein goes blames all this on the "demonization of then-new erotic commodities and services such as adult bookstores, hotel room porn rentals, thong swimsuits, swingers' clubs, mass-marketed sex toys and sexting." For instance, I think about a closeted older cousin who dispatched DVDs of Hustler's *Barely Legal* series, Private's *Sexy Gladiator,* and local Filipino *penekulas*—mainstream soft-core *Scorpio Nights* in the mid-80s and indie hardcore *Manila Exposed* in the 2000s starring Josh Ivan Morales—to his thesis advisor who would later on sexually assault him.

Miranda P. Sutton wrote a book-length extended listicle, Amazon Kindle-style, titled *My Husband Has Porn Addiction: What To Do When Your Husband is Addicted to Porn,* which pretty much explains porn addiction from the perspective of a partner. Sutton follows the premise of some authors— either non-Christians, or whose views are not centred on the mentioned religious system—on porn addiction. Such as the anonymous webmaster of NoPorn.com who wrote *Ten Keys to Breaking Pornography Addiction.* Also, the New Age-style

The Celibate Yogi's *Quit Porn Easily*, which promises to "beat the addiction forever—without the cold showers, withdrawal symptoms, deprivation and sacrifice." Tony Sayers and Noah B.E. Church, who's been recovering from porn since age 24, view porn as not a sin or gateway to eternal damnation. But as a form of addiction to the point of equating it, either stated or implied, to substance abuse disorder. Some of these books dedicate a chapter or two to the science (or neurobiology) behind the addiction without citing credible scientific sources. Thus the risk of seemingly diagnosing pathologies which might not even be exclusive to porn addiction.

The DSM-5, which recently added "gambling disorder" (under substance use and addictive disorders) and "internet gaming disorder" (for further study), doesn't say anything about addiction to pornography. None in the ICD-11 (International Classification of Diseases) as well. The DSM-5 and ICD-11, however, classify, albeit differing and wide-ranging, "hypersexual" behaviours. Called 'problematic use of online pornography' (POPU), psychiatrists from the Hospital Clínico Universitario de Salamanca in Spain came up with the following clinical manifestations: (1) erectile and/or sexual dysfunction, (2) psychosexual dissatisfaction, and (3) comorbidities including anxiety disorder, mood disorder, and substance use disorder.

I must be either bored, stressed, or lonely.

My XVideos.com search history includes: Seth Gamble in his gay-for-pay days, the dick gods Alex D. and Alex Jones, daddies Derrick Pierce and Ryan Driller, the long-dead Bill Bailey (†2019) and Denis Reed (†2016), Eric Lewis, oh god, Eric Lewis, beefcake Jake Jace, Cody Sky (or Richie Black), the now-retired Rocco Reed, Danny Mountain and his English accent, Logan Pierce (J.R. Verlin) who has a poetry collection, Danny Wylde (Christopher Zeischegg) who has a novel and a memoir, Russian Vincent Vega, Czech Ken from *Nuru Massage*, Spaniard Alberto Blanco, once a subject of one of my odes.

Recently, *Viva Hot Babes Gone Wild*, Tom Fuk, Joshua Logan, Johnny Pag, and Pinoy edging, dispatches from OnlyFans.com "porntopreneurs" and #alter Twitterverse exhibitionists, or in the words of porn studies scholars in the mid-2010s, among them Katrien Jacobs, "netporn… [phenomena of] alternative or DIY internet pornography [which are themselves] sex-positive and post-moralistic examination of digital media."

Four years ago, my right-wing country's right-wing president, known for his sexual assaults and extrajudicial killings, decided to block some major porn sites for child pornography. Four years later, without the comprehensive sex education program condemned by the "pro-life" Roman Catholic Church, rape, HIV, and teenage pregnancy statistics are still on the rise.

In the book *The Porn Trap: The Essential Guide to Overcoming Problems Caused by Pornography*, Sexologists Wendy and Larry Maltz recommends these six basic action steps in quitting porn: *(1) Tell someone else about your porn problem, (2) Get involved in a treatment program, (3) Create a porn-free environment, (4) Establish twenty-four-hour support and accountability, (5) Take care of your physical and emotional health, (6). Start healing your sexuality.*

Could I have told my long-dead Catholic grandmother that my first masturbation was to a Cosmo Philippines centrefold model whose body resembled our gardener? Is growing up in a house with two older cousins—a gay man and a bisexual woman, both still in the closet, one of them married—counted as "a porn-free environment" where there is "twenty-four-hour support"? Why does my sexuality need healing?

In the Philippines, we do not have basements to sneak into.

In his first letter to the Corinthians 6:9, St. Paul wrote, "Or do you not know that wrongdoers will not inherit the kingdom of God? Do not be deceived: neither the sexually immoral nor idolaters nor adulterers, or men who have sex with men." I am a man (a nonbinary person, actually, but does the religious right know that?). Having sex with men is sexual immoral. I will not inherit the kingdom of God. The Qur'an speaks of the same thing: it is *haram*, forbidden. I dated two Muslim guys—a Meranao who prays five times daily and an alcoholic Yakan who makes the best pork *adobo*.

A contributor from an anthology of personal narratives *Delivered: True Stories of Men and Women Who Turned From Porn to Purity* published by Catholic Answers Press, wrote this after a paragraph referencing serial killer (and porn addict) Ted Bundy as a cautionary tale:

> "[V]isual pornography (television, computer, magazines, etc.) was a male problem. Women, I was told, sometimes had 'struggles' with literature and dime-store novels—the paperbacks in the grocery store with Fabio on the cover embracing a pirate wench or a rich heiress. All those long, flowing tresses and rippling muscles—I had no attraction to those."

In 2016, several subreddits on Reddit.com applauded Filipino porn viewers. They were ranked 1st in terms of viewing duration. For their "me-time stamina," spending 12 minutes and 45 seconds watching porn (followed by South Africa's 10 minutes and 46 seconds), longer than the worldwide average. Half of them were women. Internet speed wasn't factored in.

As a pansexual, breast milk porn, stepsisters giving their stepbrothers a handjob, and femme-friendly ones where there are no necessary cumshots, no eye or breast glazed with cum, these have been some of my defining sexual awakenings. I dread fisting—someone broke up with me exactly because of that. He is currently in rehab for drug abuse.

In the same year, a study among married Filipinos found out that pornography consumption has "a positive effect on the relationship commitment in terms of satisfaction, watching online pornographic videos increase the satisfaction of the Filipino married individuals, especially on the needs for sexual intimacy."

I cannot be married or have a civil union in my country.

A local essayist I knew, once fantasized about auditioning to become a male porn star in Japan, where the porn industry needs more adult performers. He wrote this in his chapbook of humorous pieces. Streaming giant PornHub's 2019 annual review revealed that all of East and Southeast Asia prefers Japanese porn, while lesbian sex dominates in Great Britain, Australia, New Zealand, and pan-America. But this essayist and I are no longer friends. Within sexless Japan, where the law mandates that the penis be blurred onscreen, "elder" porn—two (or more) old people having sex—has been a growing niche.

Two years before he performed *hara-kiri*, novelist and playwright Yukio Mishima contributed a sadomasochistic *seppuku*-themed porn story for a Japanese gay magazine. Is porn for the suicidal a growing niche, too?

In a restroom of a movie house, I jerked off thinking about the thighs of the Amphibian Man after watching Guillermo del Toro's *The Shape of Water* with a date.

An article published in Routledge peer-reviewed academic journal *Porn Studies* found there was a lack of representation and visibility of trans-masculine and nonbinary adult performers, even in feminist adult film studios.

Whenever I watch a clip tagged in the "tranny" or "she male" categories, I think about Jennifer Laude, a Filipino woman who was murdered in 2014 by Lance Cpl. Joseph Scott Pemberton of the US Marine Corps. And whenever I think of Jennifer, I think of Pemberton and the presidential pardon given to him. I think of the Philippines-US Visiting Forces Agreement. I think of the SOGIE Equality Bill, which remains a bill after two decades. I think of the dark streets of Olongapo and elsewhere where people like me could be killed because of "trans panic."

Mine is a need to tolerate the dark wet, silent stink. A need to watch apparitions on screen just to remind me that somewhere out there, particularly in a white marble house with an overview of the beaches of Florida or mountains of California, good sex is happening. Or people pretend it does, affirming some salient collective delirium of those not getting laid because of a pandemic. In true Piscean escapism fashion, I need a fairy tale, something with a happy ending. Something predictable to make me believe that right before the end credits, orgasm surely happens.

If not, I can always replay. *Just one more, just one more.*

Alton Melvar M Dapanas (they/them), a native of southern Philippines, is the author of *Towards a Theory on City Boys* (UK: Newcomer Press, 2021). Published in Sweden, Lebanon, Germany, Taiwan, Ireland, Nigeria, Austria, Japan, South Africa, and the Netherlands, their latest works are in *Modern Poetry in Translation* (UK), *The Best Asian Poetry* (Singapore), *Mekong Review* (Australia), *Baest: A Journal of Queer Forms and Affects* (US), *Canthius Magazine* (Canada), and *Poetry Lab Shanghai* (China) where they were translated into the Chinese. They are editor-at-large at *Asymptote Journal,* assistant nonfiction editor at *Panorama: The Journal of Intelligent Travel* and *Atlas & Alice Literary Magazine,* and reader at *Creative Nonfiction* magazine. Find more at linktr.ee/samdapanas.

Bitter Pouch Cures

by Yeva Johnson

Like an opening night
fenestrated curtain, the omentum,
in all its cream-coloured magnificence,
drapes back to reveal
a secret hidden balloon
sheltering salts in a dark stew
as it floats under the hepatic lobe.
The nerve of that sneak
talking about me behind my back
hits me right in the rectus
abdominus, so that the remains
of my last great meal—
wine, bittersweet chocolate, cheeses—
lie strangled by the
common bile duct.
Meanwhile the pounding
pulse of the abdominal aorta
beats out a song demanding
Vitamin K to balance the blood.
Without this storehouse
at the pancreatic curvature
to purify gourmet feasts,

I would be without a home for my gut instinct,
left alone to carry these stones.

Renal Rollercoaster

by Yeva Johnson

For SK

No trepidation, no hesitation today, just
step right up and glide over the smooth
chestnut skin of the costovertebral angle.
Now, descend deep into the dense jungle
of the retroperitoneal adipose bed.
> Listen closely for the pulse of the renal artery
> and hold your nose at the stench of piss,
> which, even if your own, smells intolerable.
Our journey begins in the neighbourhood
of the left kidney, just under the tail of the pancreas.
A stone, a pebble, some say a nephrolith, maybe two,
sprout from the sorting and sifting magic
of one tube in and two tubes out.
> Precisely where this ride departs is unknown,
> but it's somewhere under the tight fibrous
> renal capsule. Perhaps the border control
> system that regulates how frequently
> I take my medication has gone awry.
Somewhere between the nephron
with its charge gradient and the renal cortex,
these tiny gems twist and wind their way

around the base of the renal pyramids,
playing hide-n-seek with the neural network
of impulses that signal to even toddlers,
"I have to go!" These pebbles
      feel like boulders, and when the voiding
      urge descends, pain radiates
      and I shout Ow! Ow! Ouch!
            Twin stones skip through half
            of my body's blood waste-treatment plants
            from medulla to calyx and beyond.
They scrape like the burnt rubber of a car
that slammed its brakes to stave off disaster,
and mark their trail from the pelvis to the left ureter
until finally jumping off the see-saw
      between what we ingest and what we expel,
      to plop into the bladder rest stop and provide
      me temporary respite before that final urethral exit.
Meanwhile, my left kidney continues plumbing the depths
of my bloodstream to detoxify rivers of impurities.
The vein engorges and this fountain of freshness
keeps seas of urea at bay.

Yeva Johnson, a Pushcart Prize–nominated poet and musician whose work appears in *Bellingham Review*, *Essential Truths: The Bay Area in Color Anthology*, *Sinister Wisdom*, *Yemassee*, and elsewhere, explores interlocking caste systems and possibilities for human co-existence in our biosphere. Yeva is a past Show Us Your Spines Artist-in-Residence (RADAR Productions/San Francisco Public Library), winner of the 2020 Mostly Water Art & Poetry Splash Contest and 3rd place winner of the 2022 Effie Lee Morris Literary Contest of the Women's National Book Association, and poet in QTPOC4SHO, a San Francisco Bay Area artists' collective. She was a Marion Weber Healing Arts Fellow at Mesa Refuge in 2022. Her debut chapbook, *Analog Poet Blues*, will be published by Nomadic Press in 2023.

Tendonitis

by Hayley King

shoulder blade origin
cut shallow depression
beyond deltoid tri-
angulation, supra-
spinatus strangulation
she thought
she would break
in two

she began to view pain/
as a panorama/
a landform where strata and vistas/
swallowed her whole/
broken wing dangling

it was like being
at the edge
of the Grand Canyon
all senses abducted
except for the fear
that she wanted
to fall

Hayley King is a mom, wife, veterinarian, and poet from Whitby, Ontario, which is situated on the traditional territory of the Mississaugas, a branch of the greater Anishinaabeg Nation. She completed her certificate in creative writing from the University of Toronto in 2021 and has work published in *Green Ink Poetry* and *Hags on Fire*.

Plain Sight

by Daniel Paton

INT. HOUSE, BEDROOM - MORNING

There is a lump of COVERS on a SINGLE BED. On the DESK
by the bed, an ALARM CLOCK starts RINGING loudly.
An arm pokes out from the covers, slapping the alarm clock off.

INT. HOUSE, BATHROOM - MORNING

OLLIE, 20s, stands in front of the MIRROR over a SINK. He
yawns and rubs his weary eyes.
Water starts pouring from a SHOWERHEAD. Ollie steps in the
SHOWER, his hair and shoulders quickly soaking. He shudders
from the warmth and starts to rub his face.
Something catches his attention, he looks down. His eyes are
wide. He's stunned. He wipes his face, checking again in disbelief.
We see what he's been looking at. There's a GAP where one of
the TOES ON HIS RIGHT FOOT should be.
He stares down in disbelief.

INT. HOUSE, KITCHEN - MORNING

OLLIE'S MUM, 40s, sits at the kitchen TABLE, sipping from a
CUP OF COFFEE with the NEWSPAPER out in front of her.
Ollie enters, wearing SMART TROUSERS, a SHIRT and TIE.

OLLIE'S MUM

There you are. Thought I was gonna have to
come up and get you.

He doesn't respond. Instead he goes to the FRIDGE to collect
SANDWICHES.
She doesn't look up at him while she speaks.

OLLIE'S MUM (CONT'D)

Didn't sleep at all last night. Couldn't switch
my mind off one bit. I wish I knew how to
switch it off. Do you have that problem?
Probably not, since you have the whole world
ahead of you. You don't need to worry about
things like I do.

OLLIE

Sorry, got to go. See you later.

OLLIE'S MUM

Of course, yes, see you this evening.

He leaves the kitchen.

INT. OFFICE - DAY

In a quiet office with SEPARATE DESK SPACES, Ollie stares
at the blank COMPUTER MONITOR in front of him, his
mind miles away.
CO-WORKER #1 talks at him, leaning over the DIVIDE
between desks.

CO-WORKER #1

... And then I go to him, "well what do you want
me to do about it?" cus' really, like, what can I do
about it? Like it's not even for this department
to solve really, is it?

INT. OFFICE, CAFE - DAY

CO-WORKER #2 talks to Ollie as they have their LUNCH.
Though Ollie has his sandwiches out in front of him, they remain untouched.

CO-WORKER #2

This is literally the worst hangover I've ever had in
my life... Christ it's unbearable. Should be illegal
to have to work in this state, do you know what
I mean?

Ollie smiles in response.

CO-WORKER #2 (CONT'D)

Christ... I knew those last few pints weren't
gonna be worth it. But at the same time, they
were sooo worth it... You know what I mean?
You've had nights like that right? Spontaneous
nights out are the best ones.

Ollie thinks about this for a moment, then gives an uncon-
vincing nod.

INT. BUS - EVENING

Ollie looks out of the WINDOW as a BUS rumbles down the
road. He lifts his feet up and down with apparent difficulty. His

PHONE goes off, he checks it and sees that his DAD, 40s, is calling him. He pauses a moment before answering.

                    OLLIE
                    Hi.

              OLLIE'S DAD (O.S)(D)
              Hey there, you alright?

                    OLLIE
              Yeah, um, ok, just—

              OLLIE'S DAD (O.S)(D)
            Good good, is your mother there?

                    OLLIE
                No, but I'll be—

              OLLIE'S DAD (O.S)(D)
       When you can will you get her to give me a call
          please? Cheers buddy, talk later, yeah?

                    OLLIE
                Um, yeah, sure.

The call cuts out. Ollie looks at the phone for a moment, then back out of the window.

          INT. HOUSE, BEDROOM - EVENING

Ollie stares down at his feet.
With caution, he slowly takes off the SOCK on his right foot.
There is now ANOTHER TOE MISSING—the skin is smooth and rounded where his TOES should be, like there's never been

anything there before.

He swallows a lump in his throat.

INT. HOUSE, KITCHEN - EVENING

Ollie sits at the table, a READY MEAL untouched in front of him as his Mum paces around in the background shouting down the phone.

OLLIE'S MUM

... Don't you bloody talk to me like that, I'm the one—no, I'm the one, I'm the one who has done everything the last few years. Every single thing has been on my shoulders, I haven't been able to have a life of my own because I've been looking after him! So don't you dare start...

INT. HOUSE, BEDROOM - NIGHT

In the darkness, only illuminated by the PHONE SCREEN in his hand, Ollie lays in bed.

A text message comes through from a school friend of his, LARA, 20s: "Hey, can we meet up soon? Need a good chat."

He's about to respond, bringing his LEFT HAND up to type, only to realise ONE OF HIS FINGERS is missing.

INT. HOUSE, KITCHEN - MORNING

Ollie walks to the fridge wearing GLOVES, his Mum is sat at the table again.

OLLIE'S MUM

Your bloody father wouldn't stop calling last night, he's going to be the death of me I swear. So now he wants me to...

INT. OFFICE - DAY

Ollie stares at his computer. He is still wearing gloves. He types on the keyboard, careful to use the fingers he actually has, as Co-Worker talks at him like before.

CO-WORKER #3
Every person I've spoke to today has been on me, like, I'm just doing my job here, it's not actually my fault. I can't catch a break these days, it's relentless.

Ollie goes to press a button with his RIGHT INDEX FINGER, but his hand stays motionless over the KEYBOARD. He frowns, and squeezes the finger of the glove, only to find it empty.

INT. BUS - EVENING

Ollie looks pale and sick. The bus rumbles along, jolting him. He looks across to see an OLD MAN twisting an EMPTY SLEEVE of his jacket with difficulty. The man notices Ollie staring and turns away, embarrassed.
Ollie frowns. He turns his attention ahead. He blinks heavily and looks at the man again to check if what he's seeing is real. He focuses on the BUS DRIVER, who rests his left hand on the wheel. THREE OF HIS FINGERS ARE MISSING.
Ollie can't hide his confusion.

INT. CAFE - EVENING

LARA is sat across from OLLIE, talking animatedly at him, waving her hands and arms about as she talks, but nothing is getting through to him. He watches on, not even feigning interest, but she doesn't notice.
Under the table, his shirt sleeve covers a stump where his LEFT HAND should be.

OLLIE
Are you alright, Ollie?

He snaps back into focus.

OLLIE
Um, yeah, I'm fine...

He wants to tell her. To take this opportunity to talk now that someone has finally asked about him. But the words are difficult to get out, he's not used to talking.

OLLIE (CONT'D)
Actually, I... there's something...happening, I think, I'm...not...

LARA
Hang on, one sec.

Lara slumps back, typing on her PHONE.
Ollie shuts his mouth, resigned.

INT. HOUSE, BEDROOM - MORNING
Ollie is in bed. His face is pale. He lays, eyes wide open, silent. His Mum bursts into the room.

OLLIE'S MUM
Ollie. What are you still doing in bed? It's not the weekend, you've got work soon. Come on, get up. Don't you start being as lazy as your father.

OLLIE
I can't... I'm... Sick. I'll call work.

OLLIE'S MUM

Well it's your pay that you're wasting. Just
make sure it's really worth it. You look fine to
me, though.

She leaves.
He hesitates, then looks under the duvet.
His RIGHT LEG is missing.

INT. HOUSE, BEDROOM - EVENING

In bed, still, and still wearing gloves, his face is illuminated by
his phone. Messages flood in:

From LARA: "So you know what I told you the other day, well
now guess what happened..."
DAD: "Ollie, can you put me through to your mother? She's
being difficult again."
CO-WORKER #1: "Seeing as you missed today and I covered,
I was thinking you could cover me for next week?"
CO-WORKER #2: "You're not going to BELIEVE what just
happened to me!"
CO-WORKER #3: "Bit rude of you not to turn up today
like that..."
He can't keep up with all the notifications coming through,
the PINGING sound of messages. His eyes are wide, reading
everything.
His Mum now sits by the bed, talking animatedly. He stares at
the ceiling, but she doesn't seem to care that he's not responding.
Messages keep flooding through.
There are flashes of all the gaps in his body—the smooth, round-
ed skin at his hip, his wrist, on his hand, the end of his foot.
His weary eyes blink slowly.

INT. HOUSE, LANDING - DAY

Ollie's Mum stands outside Ollie's room. She looks hesitant but heavy.

She opens the door.

Ollie is in bed, barely moving, carefully concealing his missing body parts with his duvet.

She opens her mouth to speak but then thinks better of it.

INT. HOUSE, KITCHEN - MORNING

She sits with a cup of coffee, looking ahead into space. Silence.

EXT. HOUSE, BACK GARDEN - DAY

Ollie's Mum breathes in the fresh air. She notices some DISTURBED DIRT on the otherwise flat and trimmed lawn.

She walks over to it. She pushes the upturned turf around with her foot.

She winces.

A few moments later, she walks over again, wearing GARDEN-ING GLOVES, holding a SPADE.

She digs.

INT. HOUSE, OLLIE'S ROOM - DAY

Ollie lays in bed. He seems to be half-awake, turning in discomfort. We see one of his EARS missing.

His phone sits in silence on the bedside table.

In the crack between the curtains, we can see the back garden and the figure of his Mum digging.

EXT. HOUSE, BACK GARDEN - CONT'D

Ollie's Mum has dug down about a foot.

The spade goes into the turf. She grunts and flings out more mud.

The spade ladles another pile of mud. She stops and looks at it this time. She focuses in on something in the pile.

It's a TOE—whole and healthy-looking. She gasps. Then she turns and looks at the house, up to Ollie's window.

The toe sits on the grass, a few paces away from the hole. The spade goes in again. She hits something.

She wipes some sweat off her face and looks down. She crouches and clears mud to see what it is. It looks like skin. She winces.

She follows the shape, wiping away dirt. She stands back. It's a LEG.

INT. HOUSE, KITCHEN - CONT'D

Water pours from the TAP.

Ollie's Mum washes her dirty hands and face, then dries herself with a towel.

She stands still, anxious but with a calm understanding.

Her PHONE vibrates in her pocket. She takes it out and rejects the call.

EXT. HOUSE, BACK GARDEN - CONT'D

Lay in a neat line, side by side, blemished by mud but otherwise fresh, are 2 TOES, 2 FINGERS, A LEG, A HAND and an EAR.

INT. HOUSE, LANDING - EVENING

Ollie's Mum hesitates again but then opens the door to Ollie's room. He looks up from his bed.

OLLIE'S MUM
Ollie. Darling. What's going on with you?

He shakes his head with difficulty.

OLLIE
I'm sorry... I'm not well.

She goes and kneels to him. She's willing to listen, and he's ready to talk.

INT. HOUSE, BATHROOM - MORNING

Water splashes down on the base of the SHOWER.
One foot steps in, then another. Both have a full set of toes.

END

Daniel Paton has had short fiction published in several anthologies and online literary journals, and also writes screenplays and stage plays. He currently lives in Belfast, having recently completed his Creative Writing MA, looking to work on his debut novel.

The Cadavers Speak

by Della Sullivan

Martha Owens, the coroner for Jackson County just outside Quinte Bay, Ontario, snapped on her double gloves. She stood beside the covered gurney with her arms upraised as if she was a surgeon about to perform a life-saving procedure.

Marty knew she was saying a prayer. He took the light tarp off the cold cadaver, then stood back with his legs spread and hands clasped behind his back. Taller than six feet, his posture spoke of a centurion ordered to be a witness to death. Marty observed this forty-something woman with wiry dark hair, so untameable she had lost patience and now cut it short and let nature take its course, perform her ritual. This gave him a chance to prepare for what was to come.

"Today looks like a light load, only three bodies. The first up is the old homeless woman found facedown in a pool by Denny's dumpster. No documents on her, so she is our 3rd Jane Doe this year," Marty said.

Her habit was to slowly move around the waiting bodies, squinting, appraising, humming and occasionally gasping. She would peer closely at the narrow slits of stabbing attacks, wondering aloud how such small holes could result in such an agonizing death. She would gasp at the ravage of bullet holes, especially the explosive exits. Even moles, scars, and pigment marks gave her pause.

At the pub, Marty would tell stories of how astute the coroner was. How she seemed to know things about the dead that no one else could tell. "Just by looking, she is like a prophet, telling stories of their lives, their habits and their feelings. She should have been a detective," he said.

When Martha was ready, she would nod and Marty would step up and assist her as she began an autopsy. Even law enforcement officers who wanted her opinion on the chances this was a homicide had to wait for her to work through her rituals. Nothing rushed her. Not even the time the fire alarms screamed at them. She had looked at him with one eyebrow raised as if giving her consent for Marty to leave. Then she spread her hands over the remains, silently declaring she would stay behind.

When telling this story, Marty said: "She is either the bravest or stupidest woman I have ever met. But in the face of her resolve, I stayed with her, hoping it was a false fire alarm." When his friend asked the inevitable question, he replied, "Yes, it was a real fire. It was small, easily contained and over in just a few minutes. Her only comment afterwards was that a little bit of smoke won't kill you."

No officers were present for this autopsy. Deemed an unfortunate, natural death, it was just the three of them in the large, clean room, with only two breathing. Martha handled the body gently and with awe, even after ten years of being the only active coroner in a triple-county area.

"This woman has been tremendously hurt. Her misery still surrounds her like a powerful force field, so thick nothing has been able to penetrate her heart. She has suffered. Her heart is whole but not undamaged." Martha cupped her hands, and, as she laid the heart in a basin, she made a silent plea that now she was gone, this old woman's hurt would leave her body. She shuddered to think of this lonely woman buried underneath the earth with a halo of trauma surrounding her.

"Look here," she said. "See these small, round, white scars

on her forehead and forearms. I have several just like them. They are chicken pox scars. Cigarette burns look a lot like this, but so many are sure to be pockmarks. Scars on the outside are nothing to this woman's scars on the inside. Lacerations can be terrible, terrible reminders of bad events. She smells dirty, but she wasn't a smoker. The skin on her face isn't riddled with tiny train track wrinkles, and the derma isn't thick. Her lungs are pink and plump."

Martha put on her spectacles and then looked over the top at Marty with a frank glance. "Our bodies tell our stories and smoking wasn't part of her tragedy."

Marty felt his throat close and imagined the tarry phlegm in his lungs. He vowed, that moment, to quit the filthy sticks.

"Look here on her wrists, both of them have crosswise slash marks. She cut herself many times. She didn't want to die, or she would have cut up her arm and opened up the artery. No, when she was a young woman, she cut as a way of crying out for help." Martha paused to ruminate on the ghosts of her own past. Then, startled out of her reverie by her assistant, she nodded, "Yes, all over her inner thighs, too. These marks are decades old. She has just a couple of fresh self-inflicted wounds below her knees. Once cutters get a rhythm, they rarely stop completely."

"Why would she cut herself?" asked Marty.

"Often traumatized people abuse themselves because they feel they deserve punishment. They have irresistible urges to cut. In a weird way, this makes them feel real and validated. Even as adults, they crave to be loved. This woman didn't feel wanted or cherished. She wore her scars like false victory signs."

Martha finished the procedures and motioned for Marty to sew up the 'Y' incision. "Our Jane here fell from diminished femur bones; leached of calcium, they broke into pieces. The cause of death is drowning. She is younger than she looks, probably close to sixty. There are old drug tracks but nothing fresh. Looks like she kicked her habit long ago. Her skin is dirty from rough living, and her feet are in dreadful shape, but notice her hair has been recently cut, and she has fresh polish on her long toenails. Sometime, not so long ago, she discovered her worth, and used her begged nickels and dimes to pamper herself."

"Good for you, Jane," Martha concluded. She patted the covered cadaver as Marty moved her back to the freezer wall.

The next two autopsies were on elderly men who, while in palliative care, passed from natural causes and didn't require much documentation. Martha set him free earlier than normal. "I'll finish the reports. Go have fun."

He went home and showered off the stale chemical smell from the death chambers that had seeped into his body. Feeling a trickle of expectation, he trekked down to his neighbourhood pub, running into a sudden rainstorm that destroyed his carefully constructed hairstyle. Artfully arranged and vigorously sprayed, it disguised, only to him, the fact that he was going bald. Slowly but surely, more forehead was showing, and even wearing a ball cap could not hide the rapid retreat of his hair. For a long time whenever he thought of being completely bald, he intoned an old nursery rhyme. The magic of a cow jumping over the moon still soothed him. It reminded him of his mother stroking his Scottish red locks that skimmed his shoulders. He still relished the memory of swinging his head around as a young lad. A second later his hair would swoosh around him, and remind him of the curly locks of the knight who saved Rapunzel. He equated long hair with heroism. Bald men were ugly. He cringed when he pictured himself as old. If that cow in the rhyme was touched by magic, perhaps there was still hope for his hair.

Trying to restore his hairstyle in the restroom, he leaned close to the black-flecked mirror to help guide his comb. He was struck once again at the coarse and pitted skin on his face. Until he started to work at the morgue, he stilled his essence, and tried to be as bland and invisible as possible. He was only twenty-eight, but his burden of acne still erupted, especially when he was nervous. His bad skin and pending total baldness kept him from living the adventurous life he dreamed about every time he slept alone. Thousands of nights rolled into one long spell of loneliness.

After eight months of working daily with Martha, he didn't notice he was undergoing a stealthy change in how he thought of himself. This revelation burst through his self-consciousness on this rainy day in late September when he looked closely at his reflection. In the dim light of the forty-watt bulb over the sink, he realized that the coroner was directly responsible for him discovering he had the courage tonight to ask the sweet and sexy bartender to go out with him. His broad smile showed his perfect teeth and his heart pounded faster at the thought that Beth might become his girlfriend. He didn't feel invisible tonight.

Alone since his parents' deaths during his college days, he worked as a security guard in rundown bars, or delivered for Skip the Dishes, and then ended up driving for Uber. This solitary life isolated him so much that he almost disappeared. Desperate to find more fulfilling employment, one that wouldn't keep him a hologram of his true self, but challenge his mind, the idea of working with the dead popped into his head.

He enrolled in night college courses at the regional Seneca College in Kingston. Placing his bet on human anatomy and specimen gathering, he took the class along with two older men who were dating. His professor, Dr. White Feather, was the first Indigenous coroner in the whole of Canada; a famous man, enjoying his retirement but keeping his hand in, so to speak. Although Martin was valedictorian of the class of three, he didn't attend his own graduation. His professor mailed him a decent congratulations card with a $50 Amazon gift card inside and wished him well.

With his diploma in hand, and wearing his only suit, his first job interview was with Dr. Martha Owens for the position of morgue assistant. Hunched over, and keeping his head down, he took the seat in front of her cluttered desk and peeked up to find her smiling at him.

"How lovely to meet you, Martin. You have a wonderful smile. You must be a brave and unsuperstitious soul to apply for this job. I take it, the dead don't scare you."

Her voice was like honey, warm and soothing. She wasn't pretty by normal standards, but her eyes were kind and her aura was blue. She was honest and trustworthy. Something loosened in his chest at her encouraging words and left him gobsmacked. This potential employer found him engaging and worthy, and perhaps, later, maybe even witty. At that moment, he relaxed, and the interview went so well, he started the very next day. He knew that he could confide in her, and tell her about his belief in karma and his special insights into the power of touch. He was sure he would enjoy relating his experiences of accurately foretelling the immediate future of friends and strangers who happened to physically touch him. A bit of a parlour game, but he even surprised himself with his accuracy.

He found himself relating to Martha's interpretations of the dead, and slowly found he could readily apply his budding psychic abilities and see the signs almost as well as his boss. He never got the chance to tell her how much alike they were in their perceptions.

In his fourteenth month of employment, he arrived at work and Martha wasn't there. Unusual, as she loved punctuality, but sometimes she would get held up. He puttered around, cleaned the stainless-steel tables and took instruments out of the auto-clave. He looked at the list of pending autopsies and noted their numbers in the freezer wall for quick retrieval once she arrived.

She was going to be roaring to go, talking a mile a minute about how she was steamed about a never-ending phone call, or how the road was accident blocked. Martha liked a sharp appearance and dressed up her white paper Hazmat suit with a sash of brown cloth meant to represent her hard-earned brown karate belt. On her bosom, she glued sterile plastic pictures of her pug, Bones. Every week she'd redecorate it with new pictures. Marty was looking forward to seeing this new batch of doggie love.

Marty heard the hiss of the double doors and turned to see the arrival of a new cadaver. His old college professor, a retired coroner himself, walked beside the shrouded body. A trio of homicide detectives followed the trolley, and stood silently against the doors.

"Hello, Martin," said Professor White Feathers, "today, this body takes precedence. I will be the attending coroner, and you will help me. Show me where the sterile suits are stored."

Marty opened a lab door and then transferred the body to the cold slab table. Tears overwhelmed him as he unzipped the body bag. The nude body of Dr. Martha Owens stared back at him with empty brown eyes. He quickly placed a white towel on her torso, embarrassed for her at the exposure. He turned to the professor.

"What happened?"

"That is what we are going to discover."

One of the officers said, "Her dead body was discovered by her sister. She'd been put to bed, naked, covered with a pink duvet. There was no forced entry, so she let in the killer. But her sister said everyone loved her. She had no enemies."

"She had one. She was murdered," Marty said in a gruff voice.

Marty touched her body and immediately dropped to the floor. He woke up with eight worried eyes staring down at him.

"I'm okay, I'm okay," he said, quickly rising. "Just the shock. I'll be alright in a minute."

The men stepped back to give him room. After a shaky breath, Marty put on double gloves, and aided his professor in moving the body to the autopsy table. His heart raced at the zap of cognition that crowded his brain. He gasped, but then joined as the other men bowed their heads. He shook off the unreality of the situation and stepped into the difficult task.

"May I have a couple of minutes just to get stock of this situation?" Marty asked.

He slowly walked around the body, aware he mimicked Martha, touching her shoulder and then her waist. "She has several very distinct chicken pox scars; it looks like a small burn on her left leg. A long, thin scar on the front of her right thigh, perhaps a knife. Another scar on her shoulder, ragged and raised. She made this one herself but I'm unsure how it happened."

The professor stared at Marty. "I know some of her past. She was my protégé. Those scars are very old. That raised one resulted from her being careless when roaming a neighbour's yard. She was only four when she fell into a bale of rusted wire. A nasty wound."

There was a pause as they all looked at the scar.

"She was abandoned when she and her twin sister were three and then taken into foster care," the professor continued. "Her foster mother set the kettle on for tea. When she was pouring it into her teapot, she overpoured. Some boiling water flowed over the edge of the counter and onto Martha May, playing with her sister in the cupboard just below. Her sister, Melissa Rose, was also splashed, and they were immediately taken to the hospital. Both have small reminders on their left legs. Melissa was adopted at age six by a couple from Ottawa. But they could not afford to adopt both of them. One year later, the Owens adopted Martha May, allowing her to connect with her sister. They were very good to her, and her academic side began to shine." Dr. White Feather continued his story in a low voice, "But mentally, both she and her sister suffered from depression. A lot of bad spells, until finally, well into their teens, they were diagnosed with bipolar disorder. Martha responded to her medications and was careful to avoid alcohol. She was very intelligent and able to obtain her medical degree. She married a fine upstanding dentist, but became a widow after only five years of bliss. Her sister, unfortunately, developed some bad habits. Alcohol, drugs and bad boys. This behaviour led to severe psychosis. She started cutting herself and was hospitalized when she was nineteen. Her physicians tried everything from anti-depressant drugs to behavioural modification programs. But nothing seemed to make her well."

"Melissa was always jealous of Martha and resented her success," Marty added.

"How do you know this?" asked one of the policemen.

"I sensed it about her sister when I touched her," replied Marty. "I am a bit psychotic—I mean psychic." He flashed them an embarrassed grimace and gave a small bow to the acting coroner.

Dr. White Feather began his examination. "She has strangulation marks around her neck, and there are broken blood vessels in her eyes."

"There was a brown karate belt on her bedroom floor," said the older of the two policemen. "We suspect it is the murder weapon. Because she was covered up, we believe it was someone who knew her that killed her, then wanted her to be found in a cozy, warm bed. The mark of a confused killer with signs of psychopathy."

"Sounds like it could be that jealous sister you mentioned," said his younger colleague.

"We could at least send someone out to question her." another policeman stated.

Just then, the buzzer rang at the double doors. Two gurneys and two paramedics entered the room, two bodies. One of the paramedics unzipped the first body bag, and Marty fell against the door in horror. Another Martha Owens stared back at him with empty brown eyes. The other body bag held a middle-aged man with a stab wound over his heart.

"We found them dead together. A nosy neighbour informed us that he was her boyfriend, and also the neighbourhood drug supplier,"

With trembling fingers, Marty reached out and touched the woman. "This must be Melissa Rose. I see someone robbing Martha, rifling through her wallet, taking out a bundle of bills. The foam around her mouth tells us she has overdosed, likely fentanyl, paid for with the stolen money. I see two people in a vacant house, rubber hoses around their forearms, both in difficulty. But then the woman struggles up, grabs an old knife, and plunges it into the center of the male's chest, screaming about her sister."

"Looks like you have these homicides all solved," said one of the officers. "But we still have to get busy and get proof. Good day, gentlemen."

After the long, sad day with three gruelling autopsies, Marty's brain needed a rest. He called his girlfriend and asked her out for supper. He sensed Beth would say yes. He would tell her all about how the cadavers spoke to him, and he knew she would believe him. He gave a thank-you salute to Martha for giving him courage and confidence and slowly made his way home.

Della Sullivan is a retired social worker, and lives with her husband and two enormous Maine Coon cats, in Burlington, Ontario. She enjoys her precious four adult children and seven wonderful grandchildren. She has written two novels, both still in the polishing stage, and has had three short horror stories published since 2022. She fancies herself a gourmet cook and is truly a voracious reader enjoying many genres. Her story, "A Cracked Nutcracker Christmas," was published by Jazz House Publications in 2020, in *Krampus Tales, A Killer Anthology*.

About the Editor

Catherine Mwitta is a creative writing major at Kwantlen Polytechnic University, with prior certification in Journalism from Langara College. While she isn't posting on her blog theaquilla.com, Catherine works as an editor at *Dishsoap Quarterly* and *PULP Mag*, and an editorial assistant at *Prism International*. She has short stories published in *Quarantine Reviews*, *Random Photo Journal*, *Otis Nebula*, and *PULP Mag*. Likewise, bylines at *Stir Vancouver*, *RoyalTee Magazine*, *Malahat Review*, *SAD Mag*, and *This Magazine*.

www.ingramcontent.com/pod-product-compliance
Lightning Source LLC
Chambersburg PA
CBHW072011210726
48294CB00013B/1987